About the author

Pat is a retired painter and decorator who has lived on the Northern Ireland border his whole life. He is married with four grown-up children and five grandchildren. His ambition was to write and publish his own book. He has written one book prior to this called *The Boy Who Played in the Band*.

UNMISTAKEN IDENTITY

Patrick Murphy

UNMISTAKEN IDENTITY

Vanguard Press

VANGUARD PAPERBACK

© Copyright 2024
Patrick Murphy

A CIP catalogue record for this title is available from the
British Library.

ISBN 978-1-83794-223-7

*Vanguard Press is an imprint of
Pegasus Elliot Mackenzie Publishers Ltd.*
www.pegasuspublishers.com

First Published in 2024

**Vanguard Press
Sheraton House Castle Park
Cambridge England**

Printed & Bound in Great Britain

Dedication

To my wife, Ann, and my four children who
were a constant support to my dream

Acknowledgements

I would like to acknowledge my very competent daughter, Sinead, who gave me valuable assistance in the writing and editing of this book.

Foreword

After having written my first book, *The Boy Who Played in the Band*, a lot of younger people who wouldn't have had the experience of living through the Troubles years have told me how they found it fascinating to find out how life was so different in those times. They told me they would love to know more about these times, prompting me to write this second book.

One of the greatest differences was the absence of social media back then, and this presented me with a problem of writing the book without the characters having the use of mobile phones as communication, and this might seem strange to some people while they are reading the book.

In the absence of social media, happenings during the Troubles might have taken a while to filter back to England, and because of the time delay the news could be distorted by the time it got there.

The story is based on one person's view of the British Army's presence in the North of

Ireland and how their views very quickly changed when they personally became a victim of the same Army. The book strives to show the injustices meted out to innocent people during the Troubles and how different people reacted in different ways and how this worked sometimes to their benefit and sometimes to their tragic loss.

I hope people enjoy this book as much as they did the last one. People have asked me how I ever got the Grá for writing. I would have to say that it started out at Forkhill Primary School on the Back Road, where we had a great teacher, Winnie Larkin, who has long since passed on. She would get us to write compositions and encourage us to keep it up. This is how my love of writing started. So, let's hope you all enjoy reading *Unmistaken Identity*.

Chapter 1

Tommy Grugan lay in the back bedroom in his mother's house, wondering how long this peace would last. To wake up and not be wondering whether the Brits or cops would raid wherever he chose to stay.

Today is the day after New Year's Day. A ceasefire had been called on 1st November between the Brits and the Republican movement in order to get talks going to see if there could be negotiations to end this long struggle that had taken place since the British came in here to terrorise the Nationalist Community.

Tommy had woken to the singing of a solitary bird in the back yard. The winter sun was casting a ray of light across the room. Tommy looked at his watch. Jesus, it was eight thirty, and he hadn't heard his mother Mary moving yet. Tommy had spent the evening before with his girlfriend Jenna and her family. They had a few drinks, but Jenna was adamant that he shouldn't go home, pointing out that even though there was a ceasefire they could run into a rogue patrol.

Her brother John said he'd drop him over the road, and Jenna relented.

As he lay there, he thought about this ceasefire, and he wondered: *Would the leadership negotiate strongly and not get sucked into the British twisted methods of reneging on their promises when deals were negotiated?* He wasn't entirely happy with the ceasefire, but when Tom Kane spoke to all the volunteers at the meeting in November, he assured them that just because there were people who were pushing for an end to the conflict, the Republican movement would not agree to anything less than their full demands. Most of the lads seemed happy to give negotiations a chance. For a minute his thoughts turned to how it might be something different to have a normal life. But then his thoughts went to his best mate Sean FitzGerard who was shot dead in a bloody gun battle with the Brits up at Wynne's Hill two years ago.

He then thought of his father Seamus, who had been lifted at the start of the Troubles, interned, and had contracted a lung infection while in the internment camp. Typically, the Brits left him until he was seriously ill before they released him. He didn't last twelve months after he came out. His funeral and the camaraderie of his comrades had stuck in Tommy's mind. He thought of the hundreds of people who were outside the house when they took the coffin out into the street. A large guard of honour lined both sides of the road. The Brits and police were all over the place and the helicopter hovered overhead. He remembered thinking how popular his father must have been. He remembered the man arriving at the house the next night to tell them to be out in the street at the edge of dark. The burst of gunfire could be clearly heard from the graveyard down the road. The final salute.

He thought of how his mother Mary struggled to rear the three of them and how he and his twin brother John helped the farmers after school and on holidays to get a few pounds to help her rear their young sister Meabh. How times have panned out. Meabh is married in Galway now and is just after having her first baby. John works for a security company in England. Neither could make it home for Christmas, but they are both coming this weekend, and he knew Ma was looking forward to them coming. He thought even though he and John were identical twins, how different they were. John had no interest in politics and really enjoyed his life in England with his good job, lovely house and his girlfriend Kate, who worked visiting the territorial barracks all over England as a catering coordinator. She often talked about how happy she was in her job, and it seemed as if she was very well paid. She was never in Ireland before as she thought it too dangerous with her visiting those barracks. But they said that with the ceasefire on they would take a chance.

Tommy rose, showered, got dressed and went up to the kitchen. His mother was outside hanging out the washing, so he made a bit of toast and a cup of tea. When she came back in, she told him Meabh would be here on Thursday, but John and Kate wouldn't arrive until next Monday, saying that she would have to get the house tidied. She told Tommy she couldn't wait to see Meabh's wee boy. Tommy was thinking more about Kate. Even though her parents were of Irish descent, she was a pure Brit, and with her working in the Territorial Army Barracks he worried if she would fit in around here at all.

Tommy always found the week of Christmas long, and with the ceasefire on he felt the time dragging even more. He did whatever bits and pieces that were neglected around the house with him not being about during the conflict. Time and again his mother asked him did he think it was safe to be about here, and no matter how much he reassured her, she kept asking him. He knew that deep down she wanted him around the place, but she was afraid he would get snatched by the Brits even though the ceasefire was on.

Chapter 2

That Thursday, it was just after dinner when Meabh arrived. Mother rushed out when she heard the car pulling into the yard. They threw their arms around each other when Meabh got out of the car. Mother let go just as quick and went over to the car and lifted the baby out. They both came into the kitchen and mother placed the cradle on the table, pulling back the covers to lift the baby out. You would think the baby had it rehearsed as he gave her a big, big smile. "God, he's lovely," she said. There were tears in her eyes. She cuddled him into herself. She looked over to the others and said, "It's a pity your Da wasn't here to see to see him."

"He mightn't be here to see him, Ma, but he will have the same name," said Meabh. "Ma, myself and Paul talked about names, and we decided we would call him Seamus after Daddy. You mightn't have Daddy, but you will have someone to remind you of him."

After admiring him for a while, Mary handed him to Tommy and went out to help Meabh in with her stuff. They weren't gone five minutes until the baby gave an unmerciful stretch and let a yell out of him. Tommy nearly dropped him. Tommy quickly went to find his mother, but Meabh met him at the door. "What did you do to him?" she joked. "No, just hold on to him and I'll get him a bottle. He's due one."

Tommy was glad when his mother came in and took the child off him. She sat and rocked him in her arms, but he continued to cry.

Meabh gave Ma the bottle and it was like switching off a switch when she put it in the baby's mouth. Tommy looked at his mother. She was in her glory.

Tommy helped Meabh in with the rest of her stuff. She was saying that Paul was mad that he couldn't come with her, but his da was very sick and even at his age he couldn't handle the milking alone anymore and it was hard to get help at this time of year. She said the journey up was handy enough as the roads were quiet with it being the Christmas period. She went back to see if Ma was all right with the child. Tommy continued with the few bits and pieces he was doing.

Molly Gray, their nearest neighbor, called to see Meabh and she had a present for the child. Obviously, Ma had phoned her to tell her Meabh and the baby were there. She wanted to show off her new grandchild.

Mother spent most of the day nursing the child, and her eyes lit up when Meabh asked her to get him ready for bed. Of course, Jenna arrived to see him before he was finally put down for the night. Jenna then decided she wanted to do a bit of shopping, so Tommy and her headed into town to catch the shops before they closed.

They were only around the Fairy Bridge when they encountered soldiers on the road. They seemed to have a car stopped. As quick as a flash, Jenna swung up Charlie Carey's lane, and when they pulled into the street Charlie came over to greet them. He said he had been watching the commotion on the road from the top of the steps at the loft. He said the Brits had two young fellows out of the car, and they were searching them. He couldn't hear what they were saying. Just at that moment, the noise of a helicopter could be heard approaching. It dropped in the low field. Charlie and Tommy went back up the steps to see what was going on. They were putting the two lads into the helicopter and the cop who got out of the chopper got in and drove the car away, heading for town. The chopper took off and headed in the same direction. Neither of them could make out who the two lads were.

With the coast clear, Tommy and Jenna continued on their way.

Jenna drove straight up the main street in Fairtown and Tommy knew when she turned at the cathedral, she was heading for Pennys for these boring January sales. The car park was packed, and when they did get parked Jenna was out of the car as if the shops were never going to open again. Jesus, Tommy wasn't a fan of this shopping, and with all the clothes she buys for him for Christmas, he really thought it a pointless exercise; but sure, if it keeps her happy, he'd better go along with it.

Straight away she was checking items on the shelves and gathering them up. "Look, Tommy," she said as she pulled him towards the baby counter. "This stuff will be lovely on Meabh's child."

There he was, at the till with an arm full of baby clothes – not the greatest place he had ever been in his life. At least Jenna footed the bill, because that's the only satisfaction Tommy got out of the trip.

Jenna took the short cut down Patrick Street and as she approached the Windmill Hotel, she informed him he was buying her tea. With a wry smile across to him, she pulled into the back car park.

The big open fire as you walked in the door always made the place very comfortable. They went to the bar, and he ordered a pint for himself and Jenna just wanted a Coke. They ordered off the menu and picked an empty table in the centre of the restaurant, and at that Jenna spotted Jack and Helen Lavery sitting over by the window. She spoke over to Helen and then went over to her. Jack had just gone to the toilet. Tommy knew he wasn't happy with the ceasefire. He had spoken strongly against it at the meetings. A strong republican and a great operator, he carried a lot of sway with people over the far country. When he came back out of the toilets, he came over to where Tommy was sitting.

As he stood over him, Tommy knew he was about to get a bit of his mind. "Great situation we're in now, Grugan. Us sitting with our hands tied and them cunts still patrolling the roads. Young Bailey and Hyland are after being lifted for a broken tail-light on Bailey's car. Those two boys are two good republicans and that's why they were lifted. Pure bloody intimidation. Our men gave in too handy. We should have held out for more. It's a joke. Your father would turn in his grave."

The mention of Tommy's father jolted him a little. "Jack," he said, "we don't know if this is over; negotiations are still ongoing. I'm finding it hard to settle my head, too, but we have to give it a chance."

Jenna returned to sit down, and Jack acknowledged her and returned to his table. "What's the crack with Jack?" Jenna asked. Tommy told her the way Jack was thinking. She said she could see his point and a lot of people were saying the same, but some sort of negotiation had to take place. She added that it was too early yet for people to know what was going on as there had been no news yet of the negotiations, and that was why people were confused. But it would definitely help things if the Brits weren't so visible on the roads.

Their discussion was halted when the meal arrived. Jenna said she loved coming here as the food was so good, and Tommy couldn't disagree with her. The meal was lovely.

Jack and Helen were leaving just as they were finishing off their dessert. She waved over. Jack just continued out the door without even looking over. Tommy didn't think he gave him the answers he was looking for. They finished their meal, paid the bill and left.

When Tommy and Jenna got back to the house, Meabh and Mary were deep in conversation. With the baby in bed, Mary was filling her in on all the local news. When Jenna produced the baby clothes, the conversation came to an abrupt end.

Meabh was delighted with the colours Jenna had picked. She joked that she would nearly get the child out of his cot to fit them on. Ma quickly added that one should never waken a sleeping child. They talked on for a while and Ma asked Meabh if she would like a drink? Meabh seemed surprised, but said it wouldn't be a bad idea as she hadn't had a chance to have a drink since the baby was born.

Ma went to the parlour and came back with a bottle of vodka and a bottle of lemonade she had got in for Christmas in case anyone called. Jenna piped up, "If you don't mind me staying tonight, I'll have one of them, too."

Mary smiled. "If Tommy lets you stay, it's all right with me." She fetched three glasses from the top cupboard in the kitchen, pulled over the small table from under the window and placed the glasses, the bottle of vodka and the bottle of lemonade on it. "Now I'll leave yous to it. Don't stay up too late, Meabh, you had a long journey today. I am away on down. I'll check on the baby on my way."

Meabh started talking about how it was great to be home. She said she was mad Paul couldn't come as he was sceptical about her driving the long journey with the baby, but she was happy now as she found the journey okay. She said that she was looking forward to seeing Sean, but she didn't know how to take his wife Kate, as the last time she was talking to her on the phone she seemed very distant. They discussed how she might fit in here when she comes. They talked for a couple of hours and Meabh said she was starting to feel the effects of the journey and she was going to bed. They put the glasses in the sink and went to bed.

Chapter 3

When Tommy got into the kitchen the next morning, Meabh, Jenna and his mother were already eating. Ma said to Tommy there was the makings of a fry in the oven for him. He got a plate and helped himself. Ma wondered what time John and Kate would arrive. At that, the baby started crying in the room. Jenna jumped up and said, "I'll go and get him," rushing down to the room. Meabh got up and started preparing a bottle for him. He was still crying when Jenna carried him into the kitchen. She was rocking him gently to try and pacify him, but he wasn't having any of it. When you need to be fed, you need to be fed. Jenna took the bottle from Meabh and once again, as soon as it touched his lips the crying stopped.

Tommy had just finished eating when he heard a car pulling into the yard. His mother looked out. "It's John Macken for you, Tommy," his mother said as she looked out the window.

Tommy wondered what John wanted as he had hardly spoken to him since the ceasefire.

John was a great republican; he had been in and out of prison a couple of times, but never gave up the fight. Another man who wasn't too happy with the ceasefire.

Tommy got into the passenger seat to see what he had to say. "Well, John, what's the crack?"

"Tommy, I suppose you heard about the two boys being lifted the other night. They are still in. I thought there would be none of this sort of stuff when the ceasefire is on. Sometimes I wonder, were we right having this ceasefire?"

He continued, "Tommy, our two lads were over in the Stoney field yesterday evening fishing, and just on the edge of dark the dog started scratching at a spot on one of the rocks alongside the ditch. It was whining and digging at one particular spot. Our Thomas went over to see what was wrong with the dog. It had pulled back some fabric like artificial moss. He described what he saw as a battery for an electric fence. The tiniest wire ran to a nearby electricity pole where almost at the top he could see a lens no bigger than the top of a milk bottle. He and Eamon covered the battery up again and they ran home to tell me. Tommy, that's a surveillance camera looking right into our houses.

"Tommy these bastards have us for a joke. Why would they want to be watching us when there is a ceasefire which our people are sticking to? But obviously they are not."

With this surveillance and the lifting of the two young lads, Tommy could see John was losing it. "John, settle, settle. I know you never fully supported the idea of calling a ceasefire, but we have to be careful as the talks are at a very tricky stage and if we can keep the pressure on, we don't know what we might gain. As you are well aware, the struggle had nearly become stalemate. We had to talk."

"I understand that, Tommy," John said, "but we are on ceasefire but them bastards aren't, with this shit going on."

"John, listen," Tommy said. "There's no point in us arguing about the rights and wrongs of things. I'm going to ring Gerard Dunne and we will get him to approach the local Press and we will highlight this surveillance business. Get it in the Press and show the bastards up how they are breaking the ceasefire." Gerard Dunne was the local Sinn Féin councillor who was very good at highlighting the British Army abuse. "John, the least we can do is highlight this stuff and win the propaganda war."

John sighed. "I suppose that's the best we can do, but I find it all very frustrating."

"Look, John," Tommy said, "I'll ring Gerard Dunne and we'll organise something in the next day or two. Don't say anything until we get something sorted. I'll ring you when I know what's happening."

John pulled off and Tommy wondered if he had satisfied him with his plan.

When Tommy got back into the house, Jenna was just about to go home. He walked to her car with her, and she said she would be over later. When Tommy went back into the house, Meabh and Ma had their coats on and Ma was steering the pram towards the door. They informed him that they were going for a walk up the road for a bit of fresh air, but he really knew that Ma was patrolling the road with her grandson, hoping to show him off in the chance that she might meet some of her neighbours.

With the house quiet, Tommy thought to himself, *This is the time to ring Gerard Dunne.* Gerard's wife answered the phone. When Tommy asked if he was about, she said he was outside and to hold on a minute. When Gerard came on the phone, Tommy asked him if it would be all right to call up for a crack. He said he would be there all day and joked that Tommy could help him cut the grass.

When Tommy pulled into the yard, Gerard stopped the lawnmower. They went and sat down at the picnic table. "Sorry to take you away from the work," Tommy said.

"Not at all, Tommy," he said. "You wouldn't be here unless you had important business."

Tommy told him about the surveillance camera and how it contravened the conditions of the ceasefire and how a lot of the men were very annoyed about it. He was astonished to hear the news.

He said it was bad enough the two young lads being lifted, and he told Tommy he was in contact with the police and from what they were saying they thought both of them would be released that evening without charge. He agreed with Tommy when he said they should never have been lifted. Tommy discussed with him how some of their boys were very annoyed at some of the actions of the Army since the ceasefire. He agreed that the surveillance camera would have to be publicised to the highest degree. He said he would contact all the local and national Press and, if possible, they would have a public meeting tomorrow evening in the Stoney field where the camera was situated. He asked Tommy to spread the word, and he wanted as many of their people as possible in the field. Seven o' clock would be ideal. Tommy thanked him for his help and promised to get as many people there as possible.

Tommy contacted John Macken to tell him what was happening. John said he'd tell all his friends and told Tommy to contact all his, and he would get Con Miller's lorry and it would do as a stage. He was already treating it as a military operation. Tommy got in touch with all the boys to let them know what was happening and told them to spread the word and get as many there as possible.

Tommy was just finished on the phone when Mary and Meabh came back with the baby. Meabh was smiling and she said Mary must have shown the baby to half the parish.

Ma was quick to say that if the people wanted to see her grandson, she couldn't disappoint them, and anyway, she could do what she liked with her own grandchild.

After tea, Tommy went over to Jenna's. She thought they might go into town to watch a film. The way she said it, Tommy felt he had no choice. As they got into the car, Jenna's da came out of the milking parlour. "What's going on in Stoney field tomorrow night, Tommy? I heard boys talking at the mart, but it seems to be a secret."

"Ah, no, Barney," Tommy said, "it's not a secret." Tommy told him the crack about the spy camera and how they must highlight it in the paper.

Barney seemed surprised and annoyed. "The sneaky fuckers! Seven o'clock, isn't it? Jaysus, I'll be there."

"Good man, Barney," Tommy said. "I'll see you there."

Jenna nudged him, saying that they would be late for the film.

The film Jenna picked was the worst love story he had ever seen. "The lady who finally got her man." Tommy endured it alright, he thought, until he got an elbow in the ribs to tell him to stop snoring. He gathered himself up and watched the end of it, which was no better than the start. When it was over, Jenna was up and out of the cinema like a flash. She was at the foyer when Tommy caught up with her. "Thanks for making a show of me, snoring in the middle of the film." When they got into the car, Tommy asked her if she wanted to go for a drink. The retort was, "Take me home."

When they got to the house, she just got out and went in the door. Tommy let down the window and shouted, "I'll pick you up for the rally tomorrow night." The door just closed after her.

Chapter 4

It was just after dinner the next day when John Mackin called over to tell Tommy that when John Monroe went to check on his cattle in the Stoney field there were Brits all over the place. They had two lorries over by the trees where the lads had seen the camera. "Tommy," John said, "the Press have tipped these bastards off about the rally and they have removed the camera. They wouldn't allow John into the field. When he protested, they told him there was a dangerous substance at the back ditch and no one would be allowed into the field until it was sorted. John said he had to look at the cattle. They told him they would be done by evening and that he could check on them then."

"Hold on, John," Tommy said, "I'm going to ring Gerard Dunne to see what he thinks."

Tommy spoke to Gerard on the phone, and he was adamant that they go ahead with their plans. He made the point that the people had all been told to turn up and it would be too much bother to get around them again to tell them it was cancelled. Tommy related the news to John, and he thought it made sense.

Tommy picked up Jenna at six thirty. She had mellowed a bit from the night before. Well, at least she was talking. She told him her father and mother were just getting ready to follow them. When they approached the Stoney field, they could see two lads in the middle of the road directing the cars into the field across the road. Tommy thought to himself that it was lucky it was a dry night. On entering the field, they could see there was a fair few cars already parked up.

When they got into the Stoney field, he was surprised to see the amount of people who were there. Tommy could see John had placed the lorry over by the river. Looking at his watch, he could see it was just ten to seven. Just at that moment, Tommy saw Gerard Dunne walking across the field towards the lorry. In a few minutes, Gerard got up on the back of the lorry. He lifted the loudhailer and started speaking.

"Folks, we were to start this demonstration at seven o'clock. But we weren't expecting such a turnout. So, to let everyone get parked across the road and get into us, we will delay for a short time. Bear with us. It won't be long."

After a short while when the crowd had settled in, Gerard started talking.

"Folks, it's absolutely brilliant to see such a big crowd here. For anyone not familiar with what's happening, if you look over to the trees and that little mound of earth you will see the exact spot where a British spy camera was uncovered. Now, our intention today was to remove that same camera, but someone has tipped the Brits off and they came yesterday and removed it themselves. We decided to hold this rally anyway to let you know the state of play in this area at the minute.

"On 1st November, the Republican Movement brokered a ceasefire with the British Army after lengthy and protracted talks. This was not an easy decision, with a lot of people venting their frustrations. But, as we know, the decision was taken to go ahead and cease operations to allow the talks to continue to see if we could obtain our eventual goal.

"A goal that many of our comrades have paid the ultimate price for and are lying beyond in graveyards all over the country and the countless others who are lying in jail North and South.

"The Republican Movement has stuck rigidly to the terms of the agreement, but this last while the Brits have blatantly been breaking these terms. Constant harassment of people stopped at random checkpoints which they are not supposed to be even operating. Last week,

34

they lifted two young lads up the road for no apparent reason other than a broken tail-light. Then they decide to spy on half the parish by setting up this camera. Remember, we don't know how long it has been here and it was accidentally discovered, so we would never have known it was here. So, when anyone of you are out and about, keep an eye for anything that might look out of place. You can't be up to these bastards.

"But let me tell you now. The Republican Movement will not stand for any more of these breaches of the ceasefire. Let every person take it away from here this evening. We will not be afraid to get the guns out again if they are going to take us for idiots. We are not afraid to go back to war. Good night and safe home."

There was an almighty roar and clapping of hands, and at that, the noise of a helicopter could be heard approaching. It came towards them and then hovered overhead as the people started to leave the field. Tommy told Jenna that they should take the top road home as it was almost certain the Brits or cops would mount a checkpoint with all those cars going up the road. Jenna said she'd drive, as a good-looking lass might have a better chance of charming a Brit when getting away from a checkpoint. When

Tommy looked over, he could see the wry smile on her face. He decided not to comment.

It was a good twenty minutes before they got out of the field as people in their rush to get to the meeting just abandoned their cars all over the place. It was a pure mess, with people almost losing their patience in their quest to be out the gate first. They were lucky to be close to the gate and were soon on the road home.

When they reached home, Mary was just after putting on the kettle. Tommy was parched and was glad when she poured himself and Jenna a cup each. Ma seemed unusually quiet. "How did the meeting go?" she asked.

"A very big crowd, Ma," Tommy said. "Bigger than we thought."

She leaned forward in the chair. "Tommy, is this going to start the Troubles off again? I don't want that to happen, I might as well tell you. Jimmy Tate was held on the road this evening over at the castle wall. The Brits gave him dogs' abuse. They quizzed him about you. One of them spat on the road and said that's what he thought of you." She was almost crying. Jenna looked at Tommy in amazement.

"Ma," Tommy said, trying to reassure her, "it will be all right."

"I am sick of it," she answered back. "All these years of trouble and annoyance, and as far as I can see it is going to start up again. Tommy, if they are asking about you, they are going to come and get you. What then?"

Jenna got up and went over to Mary and put her arm around her. "Look, Mary, it will be all right. Just to be sure, Tommy will come home with me tonight. They'll not find him there, and we'll look at the situation tomorrow."

Ma rubbed her eyes, lifted the cups and took them out to the sink. Tommy said to Jenna that he'd go to the room and get a change of clothes and maybe they'd head on to her house. He didn't feel too bad leaving Ma as Meabh was still there and she wouldn't be on her own.

"Right, Ma," Tommy said, "I'm away on, but Meabh will be back soon. See you tomorrow."

"Mind yourself," she whispered.

They reached Jenna's house safe and sound, although he did feel unusually nervous. They watched a film on the TV and were just about to go to bed when there was a heavy knock on the door. Jenna was startled. They could hear English accents outside. "Go to the room," she said. Tommy did as she asked. She went out to open the door and he stayed as quiet as a mouse. After a short while, she came into the room and collapsed into Tommy's arms. She was crying. "I thought they were here for you. They were laughing and asked me did I realise that my driver's window was half open, and he asked me if all Irish women were stupid. They were all laughing. Then, when I went out to close the window, one of the scumbags asked me would I like to sleep with him. The dirty bastard."

Tommy comforted her and assured her as long as they hadn't come for him, they could say what they wanted. He told her if they thought they were talking to a stupid woman they had made a hell of a mistake. They went to bed, but they didn't sleep very well. Thankfully, Jenna's Ma and Da didn't wake up down in the back room.

Chapter 5

It was Monday morning, and Tommy awoke to
the sound of chairs being dragged along the floor
in what seemed to be the direction of the kitchen.
Looking at his watch, he could see it was only
eight o'clock. He soon decided that there was no
point in lying there with all the racket going on.
Getting dressed, he went to see what was making
the racket in the kitchen. He didn't even get the
door fully open when a shout rang out to tell him
not to walk on the wet floor. Mary was in the
throes of cleaning the house and it then struck
him that it had momentarily slipped his mind that
John and Kate were coming this afternoon. He
slipped out through the back door as he knew
there was no chance of a bite of breakfast until
that floor dried. As he passed by Meabh's room
window, he could see she was standing looking
out with the child placed across her shoulder,
probably in an effort to get his wind up. She
smiled when she saw Tommy. She opened the
window and laughed. "The big clean is on,
Tommy. You'll wait for your breakfast this

morning, my boy. I was lucky. I had to get a bottle for the baby, and I sneaked a quick cup of tea. You'll be lucky to get in by dinner time."

He said he'd go to the shop and get the paper and see what way things were when he got back.

He parked at the shop and noticed John Tracy just taking down the shutters.

His wife Mary was carrying the pile of newspapers into the shop. John looked at him. "Did you wet the bed, or what has you out at this time?"

Tommy told him about Ma cleaning and about John and Kate coming home.

"John's coming home? We'll be back to this. Jesus Christ! John coming into the shop and me thinking it was you and me calling him Tommy. Sure no one can tell between you two hoors. Never mind, it will be good to see John anyway." At that, he beckoned Tommy around the back of the shop. "Tommy, I was coming to see you. Yous thought the discovery of the surveillance camera was the end of your problems. Well, these past few nights our Alsatian has started barking; and, thinking someone was going to try and rob us, I checked the cameras but could see nothing. But the cameras pick up that ditch over there at the bottom of the trees and yesterday morning around six o'clock the dog started barking. I got up and checked the cameras and just beyond that bush you can see a little gap in the whins. I copped a beret with the silver crest on it. It was only visible for a second, but I took the dog for a walk a while later and, true as Jesus, the grass was all trampled where they had been lying, and it wasn't cattle because there were no cattle in that field since Johnny Reilly died.

"The soldiers are lying there this past couple of nights. Now, Tommy, I looked from the top of the wall and there is a clear view of anyone arriving or leaving my shop, and what's more and better still, they have an excellent view of anyone leaving Wheeler's pub."

"Jesus, John, you are a good one. It's a pity we hadn't a few more like you. Keep it to yourself in case some idiots decide to take them on and get themselves killed."

Tommy continued, "Here, John, I better get what I came for and see if I can get a bit of breakfast. Thanks for that." He paid for the paper and headed home, puzzled by his new bit of news.

Driving home, he was thinking how sound a man John Tracy was. He was even selling the *Republican News* in the shop until the Brits came into the shop and tore all the papers up and thumped John around the place and told him he'd get worse if he ever sold it again. He was adamant he wouldn't stop, but they had to advise him otherwise.

When Tommy got home, the kitchen was clear as Mary and Meabh were taking the sitting room apart. Tommy put on a bit of toast and thought it better to stay clear of the cleaning ladies. The front page of the paper was covered with pictures of the protest they had over at Stoney field. Thankfully, there were none of himself and Jenna, but her mother and father weren't so lucky as they stood out in one of the pictures of the crowd. At that, the phone rang and mother came into the kitchen and said John and Kate had landed at the airport and they were organising a hired car and they should be with them in an hour.

When Tommy finished reading the paper, he thought he had better spruce himself up a bit in order to impress the English woman. Meabh had taken the child into the kitchen to change him into a different outfit. "Must have the wee man looking well for his aunt and uncle," she said, smiling at Tommy.

"I must get myself sorted," Tommy said.

"You'll be lucky," Meabh said. "Ma is in the bathroom and by the time that she's finished the folks could be here."

When the child was dressed, she handed him to Tommy. He was smiling up at him as he got engrossed in his antics.

He realised from the noise of the lock engaging on the bathroom door that she had only given him the child to get to the bathroom before him. What a chancer. After a while, his mother came in to take the child as she had a bottle ready for him. "Need to get this little man a bottle and a wee sleep so as he will be in good form when John and Kate arrive." She was dolled up as if she was going to a wedding.

It must have been half an hour when Meabh came out of the bathroom. "Tommy, you can go in now," she said with a wry smile. "Thanks for minding the child."

Tommy wasn't long showered and dressed when he heard a car pulling into the yard. He made his way down the hall, but when he got to the back door Ma and Meabh were already out in the yard. He could see the black Mercedes. The two doors opened simultaneously, and John and Kate got out. Ma ran and threw her arms around John, and he lifted her clean off her feet. Meabh went over and hugged Kate. Ma couldn't control herself and she was crying when John put her down. She went over then to hug Kate.

John came over and put his arms around Tommy. "Great to see you, Tommy," he said.

"And you, too, John," Tommy answered. "It's been too long."

Kate approached and Tommy gave her a hug. She said it was so funny to hug someone who looked so much like her husband. Tommy laughed, telling her she got the best twin.

They all went into the house, and Ma still had tears in her eyes. She lifted the towel and dried her eyes, asking Meabh to put on the kettle. Kate went straight over to the pram to look at the child. She called John over. "Isn't he just lovely, John? Maybe someday we will be blessed with a child of our own, and if he's half as nice as this wee man he will be beautiful."

"I can't get over you called him Seamus after Da, Meabh," John said. "It's just brilliant. If he's half the man Da was, he will be some boy." They could tell John was very happy the way he looked at the child as he spoke.

Mother had the tea on the table, so they all sat down and the chat started. It went from how Meabh and Paul were doing in Galway, to how John and Kate were doing in England, to how well Ma was looking. Then Kate dropped the clanger, "We really knew we had to come over this Christmas. John was so mad to get home to see you all, and then when the IRA gave up we knew it was time to go. Everyone at home is so happy that they have gone away."

44

Silence for a second. Ma jumped up and gathered the cups, Meabh jumped up to look at the child, John showed no emotion.

Kate continued, "John never talks much about the goings-on over here, but when you listen to some of the soldiers who served here and they tell about how some of their comrades met their end, there must be some very vicious people in the IRA."

Tommy's blood was boiling, and he was just about to explode when Meabh opened up. "Kate, you know nothing about our situation. Around here, all the people wanted to do was to live in peace and make a few pounds. Then the Brits came and raided the houses of innocent people, lifted some of them and put them in prison camps like my Da. My Da contracted serious lung disease and was left in jail until it was too late to cure him when he got out. My da was nothing but a gentleman. He had no interest in politics."

"That's enough, Meabh," Mary butted in. "Kate, I know you're English, but we didn't fall out with the English – we only fell out with the uniform. My husband died far too young because an English soldier decided he was a terrorist. My husband hadn't even a driving offence. You and John are happily married, and I hope you have a long, happy life; but let me tell you, it's very, very hard when you lose your husband at a very young age, especially when he had done nothing wrong. So, from now on I think we should all be careful before we open our mouths. We are all a family and need to get on. You are on holidays, and I want yous to enjoy it, so I've said my piece."

"Mam, I am probably to blame," John butted in. "I never said anything to Kate about what went on around here. I told her about Da, but I never went into any detail. I know by her reaction she is surprised. All she ever hears is through the British media."

"John, it's over," Mary said. "Now, I have you two, Tommy and Jenna and Meabh booked into Hoey's for a meal at eight o'clock. So, gather yourselves. I am going to mind the baby."

They all looked at her in amazement. "But, Ma," Meabh said, "are you not coming, too?"

"No, I booked it yesterday for you all to give you a chance to get out together; and anyway, I want to have the child to myself for a few hours."

Jesus, Tommy thought to himself, he'd better call Jenna so as she can get organized, thinking, *I'm glad now that I didn't open my mouth earlier. Ma and Meabh did a great job on their own.*

Jenna was surprised that Ma had booked a meal for them, but added that she'd take a free meal any time. Tommy told her he'd pick her up at a quarter to eight.

Meabh seemed very excited at the idea of getting out for the evening, knowing that the baby would be safe in Ma's care, and she always liked being with John and Tommy since she was a child. She probably used them as a substitute for Da since he passed on. At that, Meabh suggested that they should ring 'Taxi' O'Hara and get him to pick them all up and then they could go for a couple of drinks after the meal and could ring him to pick them up and take them home.

"Here, I'll do it," she said, heading into the hall to the phone. Taxi's real name was Micky, but everybody called him 'Taxi' because of his occupation. Meabh then went over to where Ma was holding the baby. "Ma, will you make sure you get all his wind up, or otherwise he'll not sleep through the whole night?"

Mother retorted quickly, "Do you think I never winded a child before? I winded you all of them years ago and there was never much wrong with you."

Meabh smiled and kissed the baby on the forehead. "Your Nanny will take good care of you."

A short time later, they heard the honk of a horn out in the yard. They all headed outside, and

Tommy opened the door of the minibus to let the rest in; but on seeing John, 'Taxi' jumped out and came around the minibus. He caught John's hand and shook it briskly. "John Grugan. Jesus, I heard you were home, and is this your good lady?" He shook Kate's hand and kept hold of it while he continued, "Jaysus, you done no harm in England finding a good-looking woman like this, then letting go her hand to her relief. And, Meabh, congratulations on your new arrival. You're looking great, too."

Tommy reminded him that they had a meal booked and they still had to collect Jenna.

"Ah, Jaysus, Tommy, will you give over! I don't know the last time I saw your brother. We'll get there in time."

Tommy hopped in the front and the others got in the back. When they reached Jenna's, 'Taxi' beeped and Jenna came straight out. Tommy opened the front door and she got in beside him. 'Taxi' started up again. "Jaysus, Jenna, you are looking well. This fellow of yours is panicking we'll be late. I wonder will he be as quick up to the bar?"

"Maybe not, Taxi, we'll see," she answered.

They reached Hoey's with no time to spare. Meabh told 'Taxi' they would give him a ring when they wanted him to take them home. He told them to have a good night and drove off.

When they went into the restaurant, the manager directed them to a table up beside the old window which had been retrieved from an old church that had been demolished to make way for new houses over in Creanstown, which ironically now is called Church Avenue. It allowed a lot of light into the restaurant. The waiter was quick to come with the menus, and after a while he returned to take their orders. Tommy and Jenna stuck to their usual steak sandwich. Meabh went with Chicken Maryland. Kate asked what the pork was like. Tommy said he couldn't be sure, but he had never gotten a bad meal in this place. She and John settled on Pork.

Tommy always liked Hoey's because of all the old antiques they had in glass cases on the walls. It made the place very homely. Kate was amazed by the place and after looking at all the stuff on the walls, she asked, "What are those two items each side of the fire?" Meabh proceeded to explain that one was an old churn which had been used for churning milk to make butter. "But how did it work?" Kate asked.

"You just poured in the milk and kept turning the handle and the tumbling of the churn turned the milk into butter," Tommy said. Kate looked puzzled.

"And that one on the other side is an old bellows," John added. "It was alongside the fire, and you just turned that wheel, and it caused a draught which caused the flame to get the sticks to light and get the fire going." Kate looked amazed.

At that, the food was about to be served. Everyone got their choice. Things were pretty quiet while everyone tucked into their grub. Jenna was finished first, as usual, saying how much she enjoyed the meal. John and Kate said they thought the pork was lovely.

Meabh said she was looking forward to the dessert menu. She hadn't the words out of her mouth when the waiters had come to clear the table, handing everyone a Dessert menu.

Tommy declined as he said he was full enough and would abstain. There was a special of Apple Crumble and Ice Cream, and they all went for that. Then they all finished off with a cup of tea, sitting for a while just to savour the food they had just eaten. Tommy made an excuse to go to the toilet, and on his way back went to the cash desk and paid for the meal. He thought it was the least he could do with Kate and John not being here for so long.

Meabh was getting fidgety and suggested they head on over to Wheeler's for a drink. John said he was getting up to ask for the bill, but Tommy informed him that the meal was paid for. Both John and Kate were mad at what he had done. But Meabh chipped in, "Seldom's wonderful."

They took the short walk to Wheeler's. They picked a table down at the back. John headed towards the bar, saying as Tommy had paid for the meal, so he was buying the first round. John knew Tommy and Jenna's drink and he knew his and Kate's, but he forgot to ask Meabh. He went over to ask her what she wanted. She said to get her a gin and tonic. They took the drink back to the table. The conversation split in two, with the girls engrossed in their own conversation and Tommy and John making up for lost time. John told Tommy how he and Kate were very happy and had been trying to start a family, but they hadn't had much success so far. He said Kate was a bit anxious when she saw Meabh's baby as she really wanted one of her own. He asked was there any sign of Tommy and Jenna getting married? Tommy explained to him that when the Troubles were on, the situation was very tense and he never knew where he would be at any given time. It wouldn't be fair to put a girl in a position where he could be arrested or worse and leave her on her own. Tommy told John that he and Jenna had discussed marriage and they both thought they would wait to see how this ceasefire worked out.

John said he hoped that it went well, that it was better to be at peace than living your life looking over your shoulder all the time.

"Yes, John," Tommy said. "That's okay if things were normal. But if the Brits don't pull back, it is no good. These last few years we have been living looking down the barrel of a gun every time we turn a corner. There are too many men dead or in jail to back down now. The Republican movement has stuck rigidly to the terms of the ceasefire, while the Brits have been breaking them every day."

John sighed. "Tommy, I only want to see you having a bit of a life. It can't be easy having that stress on your shoulders all the time. Anyhow, let's change the subject. You quit playing the football; why was that?"

"I couldn't commit on a regular basis," Tommy said; "and if you can't be there all the time, it's no good to the club."

At that, the girls got up to get a drink. When they returned with the drinks, they headed to the loo. When they returned to the table, Tommy knew Jenna was livid. "What's wrong?" he asked.

"When we were standing in the corridor after coming out of the toilets, that nuisance Jimmy Brady told Kate that English people weren't welcome here," Jenna said.

Kate was very annoyed. "Meabh was going to go for him, only I stopped her."

"I wish you had let me," Meabh said.

"Maybe we should leave," Kate said anxiously. John looked at Tommy, puzzled.

"Wait a minute," Tommy said. "There's nobody going anywhere. If a jumped-up little toe-rag like Jimmy Brady is going to put me out of my local pub, I may as well lie down and die. The same boy, if he saw a Brit within five hundred yards of him, he'd wet his trousers. Here, just sit down and enjoy your drinks, girls; I'll be back in a minute."

When Tommy returned, they had all settled down a bit. "Now," Tommy said, "we'll have no more trouble with that Mr Brady; the session's on, get it in to you." Kate looked a lot happier.

It was well into the early hours when they rang the taxi. When 'Taxi' pulled up, they all got in and Jenna told him that her and Tommy were going to her house and the rest were going home. Tommy didn't know that was the plan, but who was he to argue? 'Taxi' said for some reason there were a lot of help (Brits) about.

His own way of telling them to be on their guard. He felt better now that he was staying with Jenna. They got out when they arrived at Jenna's. Tommy went to pay 'Taxi', but he told him

Meabh had it sorted. They said their goodbyes, telling them they'd see them in the morning.

Chapter 6

The next morning, they were just having breakfast when Jenna's da came into the kitchen. "There's a lot of activity about whatever is going on. I saw them crossing the gate into Tolan's field and continue along the march ditch heading for the low road, and when I went in for the paper, John Tracy told me they were stopping on the main road early this morning and lifted a couple of boys on their way to work. They are certainly not paying any heed to the ceasefire. If you want a lift home, Tommy, I'm going over to look at the cattle behind your house. If you jump in the cab of the tractor, we can go most of the way across the fields."

"That will save you having to leave me over," Tommy said to Jenna. "I'll give you a ring later on to see what we'll do tonight."

Tommy and Barney headed away on the tractor and when they rounded a sharp turn there was a checkpoint. Not one to panic, Barney turned in a gap into the field. Smiling, he turned his head and said, "Sometimes it pays to leave your gate open."

Heading across the field, they could see soldiers lying at the back of the ditch covering the checkpoint. Tommy jumped down from the cab and opened the gate that took them onto Rickety Lane, and this would lead them within one hundred yards of Tommy's house. Two fingers to that checkpoint. Barney was questioning why there was so much activity about, and it was going through Tommy's own head what was going on. Barney pulled up at the end of the lane and Tommy told him to go on left and check the cattle, as he would walk the short distance to the house. He jumped down from the tractor and headed on home.

He wasn't twenty yards down the road when an unmerciful bang nearly knocked him off his feet. What the hell was it? He was kind of stunned as he knew that bang wasn't too far away, but when he steadied himself he ran like hell for the house.

When he got to the house, he burst through the back door. Everyone was peering out of the window. He could see the fear in their eyes. Meabh was clutching the baby close to her chest. John was holding Kate and she was crying. Ma appeared out of the room with the rosary beads clutched between her fingers. "Jesus Christ,

Tommy, what's going on?" she said. "What's going on?"

"What's happening?" Kate screamed. "I want out of here."

Meabh stared at him. "Listen," Tommy said, "I know no more than yous do. Keep calm. Whatever has happened has happened. Settle down and I will try and find out what is going on. Sit down, sit down. I'll make some tea."

Ma, knowing that this wasn't his forte, went over and put on the kettle.

The roar of the choppers could be heard overhead. Tommy went out to the back to see if he could see anything. There was a large plume of smoke. He thought to himself, *What the hell is going on? Phoning is out of the question. Jesus, is Barney safe on the tractor?* Jesus, it struck him like a flash of lightning. There was a landmine buried close to where that checkpoint was. Something had detonated it – or someone!

Jesus, have some of our boys broken the fucking ceasefire? He went back into the house.

Mary knew he was puzzled. She handed him a cup of tea. "Tommy, I know you are surprised at this, but is this the bloody whole lot started up again?"

"Look," Tommy said, "I told yous, I know no more than yourselves about this. I won't be able to find out anything until things settle down."

Kate butted in, "We could have been killed. I knew we shouldn't have come here."

John looked like he was too afraid to open his mouth. The tension was broken when wee Seamus screamed out below in the room. Mary and Meabh both went to tend to him.

At that, Tommy heard a tractor pulling into the yard. He looked out and saw Barney coming to the back door. When he came in, he looked at him with a kind of a smile. "Are you trying to get me killed? That bomb nearly blew me out of the fucking tractor. I got back through the fields lucky enough. Paddy 'The News' Wilson [John Wilson got his name from being so nosy] stopped me just as I came into the yard. He could tell me that there were four soldiers killed in that bang and several more injured. So much for your ceasefire, Tommy boy," he laughed.

Kate said, "Why are you laughing? Those people have relatives and friends. It's a disgrace."

"So had my grandfather when he was shot down in Kileck all those years ago," Barney retorted. "We never sent for them damn soldiers and we have to let them know we don't want them."

Mary heard the commotion from the room. Rushing into the kitchen, she shouted, "Barney, shut up. Kate is terrified. She doesn't understand all this. We had the Troubles, and we know people were killed and injured on both sides. I know all about losing my husband and this boy here having to stay away from home for long periods of time, but we thought it was bloody well over when we got the ceasefire. We thought it was time to get an agreement, and now it seems someone has gone and messed it up. We can't figure it out." There was silence.

Barney seemed in an awkward position. Tommy saw his chance. He said to Barney, "Come on, Barney. I need to see someone. They are less likely to stop a tractor than a car." He could see Barney was glad of a quick exit. They avoided the scene of the explosion and Tommy asked Barney to drop him over to John Macken's. He needed to make some sense of what had happened. When he went into the yard, he could see John in the shed across from the house. He peered around the doorway and, seeing it was Tommy, he came to meet him. "I was just going to contact you, Tommy. What the fuck's going on? Is there something yous are not telling me? Are we not all in this together? What's going on with this explosion?"

"Stop, John! Stop!" Tommy said. "I don't know any more than you. I am just as baffled as you at the whole thing."

John then told him he had rung Jack Lavery and he was on his way over. Maybe he was on his way over, but they both knew that Jack would have a different view about things than them because he wasn't at all happy with the ceasefire.

Tommy and John were mulling over what might have happened when Jack's car pulled into the yard. He came into the shed and shut the door behind him with a smile on his face. "What's up with you two? Don't tell me yous are in bad form over the explosion."

"Jack," John said, "we have no more love for the Brits than you, but we were prepared to stick to the conditions of the ceasefire until we heard different. God knows where this will bring us now. We'll have to meet with the boys from the far country and see where we go from here. There were only a few people knew that mine was there. Could it be that it was accidentally detonated?"

"Not a chance," Jack said. "The man that put it there would make sure that couldn't happen. And anyway, the three of us are aware that there are a lot of lads that are fed up with the Brits getting away with all sorts of stuff and we are sitting back with our hands tied."

At that, there was a rap at the door. John went over and opened it, and they could hear his wife Mary telling him there was a phone call for him. "You know, I think some of the younger lads are behind this," Jack said. "There's a lot of them getting harassed and lifted and not being able to retaliate."

"But, Jack, orders are orders," Tommy said, "and they must be adhered to. We'll see what the boys over the far country will have to say."

At that, John came back. "Well, boys, the shit has hit the fan now. That was Grisly on the phone. We have to be at the old farm tomorrow night. I have to contact the four other boys."

Jack smiled. "We are going to get our knuckles rapped for a successful operation we weren't even involved in."

John seemed annoyed. "Keep it for Grisly, Jack," he snapped. "And it might be better to not be at home tonight. I'll run you home, Tommy."

When Tommy got home, his ma told him that Kate and John were trying to book a flight home, as not only was Kate mad to get out of there, but she emphasised that she would never be back. The atmosphere was rather tense all evening, but fortunately his mother was preoccupied with baby Seamus. At one stage, Meabh followed Tommy outside. She talked about how everything had changed so quickly. She said,

"Things aren't being helped with Kate continually going on at Ma and trying to blame you for everything. It's going to be harder on you than any of us. This is putting everything back to where it was, isn't it?"

"It's hard to know, Meabh," Tommy said. "I'll know better tomorrow night."

"Jesus, please be careful, Tommy."

"Ah, I'll be all right, Meabh. I'll stay over in Jenna's for a couple of nights to see if they are raiding."

"I'll stay another couple of days with Ma to see how things work out," she added.

Tommy tried to keep away from Kate because she was doing everybody's head in about getting out of this damn country. That evening, Tommy contacted Jenna to let her know he would stay over in her place that night.

Chapter 7

The next day, it seemed like no time until he had to head to the old farm for the meeting. He drove down to the supermarket car park where John was waiting so they could both travel together. When Tommy got in, John told him he had just contacted the scout car and the area was clear.

After about twenty minutes, they were in the yard of the old farm. When they went inside, Jack Lavery was already there, and Grisly and his trusted sidekick Vincy were seated at the top of the old round table. The atmosphere between both parties seemed tense. Jack never had much time for hierarchy. The other four boys all came in shortly afterwards.

Grisly started. "Thanks for coming, lads. I know there is a lot of security about, but it's important to have this meeting. What happened the other night was definitely not our plan, but we have to try and figure out what will the Brits' reaction be to it. We have already investigated the whole situation and we have found out that two young volunteers who had been getting harassment decided stupidly to take the law into their own hands."

"I think they were right," Jack Lavery butted in. Tommy shuddered, as Grisly didn't take kindly to people butting in.

"There were far too many harassments and arrests when there should have been none," Jack added. "Was that not in the Agreement? Maybe these young fellows were right and us older men are getting too complacent."

Tommy knew Grisly wouldn't take much back chat and he hated to be interrupted. He suddenly stood up and hit the table with his fist. "Jack, I didn't come here to listen to you criticising the movement. Everyone active in this movement does their best no matter what age they are." He scowled at Jack. "I am a bit older than you and I hope you are not implying that I am not doing my job right."

Vincy indicated with his hand that he wished to speak. Grisly nodded for him to go ahead. "Boys, it's all right saying that these lads were right, but they broke an International Agreement. When the Republican Movement gives its word to something it likes to keep it, otherwise you'll not be believed the next time you give it. Now, we know the unrest a lot of volunteers were feeling, and the Agreement mightn't have lasted that long more anyhow, but we would have liked to end it on our own terms, not like this."

Grisly started again. "We don't know if the Brits will react and leave us in no man's land, because we can't predict what they will do. We have to talk to the negotiators tomorrow to try and judge the next move."

Out of the blue, one of the other four lads asked, "What will happen to these volunteers who broke the rules?"

Grisly sighed and shifted from side to side on the chair. "That will be up to the boys at the top. The way I look at it, something like this incident was on the verge of happening anyway because of how the Brits were pushing our people to react. The fact that the operation was such a success, those who carried it out will have a feather in their cap, and to get rid of them could mean them going their own way. That would mean we would no longer have control of them. We all know that frustration can make anyone change, and it seems this is what has happened.

"Now, we needn't hang about here much longer. We will be meeting the big boys tomorrow and we will let yous boys know what the state of play is. Now the Brits aren't going to take this lying down. Yous would want to stay offside and be careful where you go. Treat things like we did before the ceasefire.

"We will leave ten minutes apart to avoid undue attention." Looking over at Tommy and John, he said, "You two boys go first, and we'll be in touch with you."

Tommy and John were discussing the meeting on their way home, when they saw a white car flashing its lights. When they got up beside, Tommy recognised his cousin Ann Brobhy. John wound down the window and Ann said, "God, John, I'm glad I got you and Tommy stopped. The Brits are back up the road there. They have a coach stopped and they have everyone out on the road."

"Jesus, Ann, Thanks. We'll turn round now," John said. With Ann gone past, they turned to warn the others to take a different route. "Jesus, we were lucky there, Tommy," John said. "Them boys would just have loved to get a hold of us two. It would definitely be a seven-day stay locked up, or worse. Especially after them losing four in that explosion."

They eventually got back to the supermarket and John dropped Tommy off. The helicopter had been an ever-present since yesterday. It had just passed overhead as Tommy travelled along the road. He could see it had dropped down in the meadow. He should make Jenna's before they make it to the road.

He pulled into Jenna's and drove the car straight into the hay shed so that it couldn't be seen from the road if the soldiers passed. He knocked the back door as he thought there might be no one at home, but straight away Jenna's mother Jane opened the door. "Ah, Tommy, you got back okay. There's been some activity around here all day. I was wondering, would you get back at all? Here, I'm only after making a pot of soup. You'll join me for a bowl. Come on."

They had barely finished when the door opened, and Barney came in. "Something smells good about here. I'll have a drop of that soup, Jane you girl. Jesus, Tommy, you're getting your feet under the table about here, even sitting in my seat at the top of the table." Tommy quickly moved to another seat. He was smiling to himself. "You'll be back here tonight again, Tommy?" he said. "Jimmy Teelan was lifted at two o'clock this morning and they pulled Jimmy Payne's house apart around six o'clock this morning.

"I think he got a bit of a beefing along with that. I was talking to Tommy Rafter down at the grain store, and he said he heard the chopper landing around six and he said they were down for a good while. They took Jimmy with them."

Barney had collected a load of meal from the grain store and Tommy said he would give him a hand to load the meal into the shed to try and pass the time until Jenna got home from work. He had other bits and pieces to do around the yard and he was glad of the extra pair of hands. Everything was going well till they heard the English voices behind the wall. Tommy rushed across the yard to the hay shed, ran up the ladder to the top of the hay bales, pulled the ladder up after him and hid at the back of the bales. They saw Barney in the yard.

"All right, Grandad, how's the farming going?" Tommy could hear the Brit saying.

"Ah, Jesus gasson, it's a fucking struggle. The price of cattle to buy. The low price when you go to sell them, the price of meal to feed them. Then if they get sick the price of vets and medicine.

"Do you know, young man, that you are a very lucky man that all you have to do is walk around the roads and get paid for it, and you're always with your mates and can have the crack? Jesus, sometimes I wish I had to join the British Army." Tommy almost laughed out loud.

The soldier started, "It's not that easy. It wasn't easy for my four mates the other day. They were killed."

"I heard something about that," Barney said. "That's one thing I'd have to learn if I joined the

British Army. Keep your eyes open and keep your head down."

"Are you taking the piss?" the soldier asked.

"Jesus, not at all, son," Barney said. "Not at all. Like most people around here, I am a catholic and I was on my bended knees praying for them fellows."

Thankfully, Tommy heard Jenna shouting that there was someone on the phone for him. Tommy stayed where he was until Barney let him know the soldiers were gone.

Tommy put the ladder back in place and climbed down. He looked at Barney, who had his usual grin. "You talked some bullshit to them boys," Tommy said. Barney started to laugh. "I nearly believed it myself."

Barney was still laughing. "If you keep them boys in conversation, they forget what they are about."

Just at that, Jenna drove into the yard. She got out of the car and rushed over to them. She looked at Tommy and said, "Do you know the soldiers are just down the road?"

"Ah, we had them," Tommy said. "Your father was teaching them how to stay alive. He even told them he might join the British Army."

Once again, Barney had a smile on his face.

"And where were you when this was going on?" Jenna asked, staring at Tommy.

"Up behind those bales, thank God."

"Come on," she said. "We'll see what mother has for dinner." Barney headed back into the shed.

Chapter 8

After they had their dinner, Tommy asked Jenna to run him over to his Ma's. She was glad to see him. She said she was worried about him as Mary Lavery rang to say Jack and John Macken had both been arrested. Tommy told her that he would stay at Jenna's for another while. She said John and Kate had gone into town with Meabh. John wanted to buy Meabh her tea as they had re-arranged their flight home.

"They're leaving in the morning. I am glad in a way," Ma said, "because Kate hasn't stopped going on about wanting to get out of this place and how she never will be back. John just seems to accept anything she says. I'd rather mind the child anyway."

Tommy wondered what Ma would do when Meabh went home. She was definitely going to miss wee Seamus. Ma made a drop of tea, and it wasn't long until they heard a car pulling into the yard. Tommy got up and looked out the window and as he thought, it was John and the two girls. He noticed Kate was driving. When they came in,

Meabh said they had eaten in Keenan's, and it was lovely. Kate said it was her last meal in Ireland and, as usual, John just looked at her and said nothing.

"I hear you are heading away in the morning," Tommy said to John.

"Yeah," he said. "Kate isn't settled at all, and I think it's better to go. We'll only miss two days of our holidays. Every time we have to go through a checkpoint, she shivers with fright. We went through a checkpoint down outside Tom McCann's house yesterday and the soldier talking to us thought I was you. He examined my licence up and down and he was going to arrest me, only that Kate said who she was and where she worked.

"She didn't sleep last night thinking about it. Kate has done the driving since, as she thinks they won't give her as much hassle."

"It'll not happen again," Kate butted in, "because when I get back to England, I'll not be back."

Tommy noticed his Ma giving her a dirty look. She was really annoyed with her. They talked for a while, and Tommy heard a car pulling into the yard. Jenna had come back to collect him. When she came in, she said she had come through a checkpoint down the road, and they would have to go home the back road.

When Tommy told her John and Kate were going home in the morning, she was surprised. "Ah, that's a pity," Jenna said. "I thought we might have had another night out before yous went home."

John teased Jenna that if there were wedding bells they would return. Kate once again butted in, "Things would want to change a lot, or you'll be coming on your own."

They said their goodbyes as they wouldn't see them again. They would be leaving early in the morning. Tommy and Jenna headed on. Ma shouted after them for Tommy to ring and let her know he was safe.

Chapter 9

Kate and John were pulling out of the yard at exactly a quarter to seven. Once again, Kate said she would drive as she might get through a checkpoint handier. They hadn't gone too far when they came on a checkpoint. The soldiers had a black van stopped and two lads were standing on the road. The soldiers seemed to be arguing with them. Another soldier was searching inside the van. Kate was wondering if they would be held up for long as they didn't want to miss their flight. After a short time, the boys in the black van were allowed to go. When they got up to the checkpoint, they were beckoned to stop. The soldier asked Kate for her licence. He looked at the licence and then at her. "Where are you going this time of morning?"

"We are going to catch a plane," Kate answered. At that, he glanced in at John. He walked around to the passenger side and opened the door.

"Thomas Grugan, can you step out of the vehicle?"

John said he wasn't Thomas Grugan. The soldier pulled him that hard that he fell onto the ground. The soldier caught him by the throat. "Do you know that four of my mates were killed by you bastards the other night?" John protested that he wasn't Thomas Grugan. The soldier was kicking John on the ground. Kate got out and screamed at the soldier to look at John's licence. John managed to get up and showed the soldier his licence. "You are all the fucking same around here," the soldier said. "You two get the fuck into that car and get to fuck out of here."

Kate was shivering. She got in quickly and drove off. She had hardly got into top gear when she heard a loud noise. John fell to one side against the passenger window. She shouted at him what was wrong. There was no answer. He slumped into the footwell. He had gone a very pale colour. She pulled in and went to get out of the car when she noticed blood seeping through the sleeve of her own cardigan. She was bleeding. She continued around to John. He wasn't moving. She called his name, but there was no response. She went to shake him, but when she put her hand on his chest, she could feel the blood. Her hand was covered in it. *What will I do?*

At that, a car pulled up. "Are you all right?" asked the driver.

"I think we've been shot," she said.

The man jumped out. He pulled up her sleeve. "You have a right hole in your arm."

"Don't mind me," Kate screamed. "My husband isn't responding."

The man ran around to John. He felt his pulse. "He's still with us. Look, get into the back of the car and give me the keys and I'll drive you to the hospital. We have to hurry."

Kate kept talking to John, but there was no answer. The man couldn't drive any faster. When he got to the door of outpatients, he jumped out and shouted to an ambulance man that there was an emergency. The ambulance driver spoke on his walkie-talkie and minutes later two nurses came running towards the car with a trolley. The ambulance driver was already tending to John. He quickly had him placed on the trolley and rushed to the hospital entrance. Kate and the man who helped her followed them into the hospital. The man led her to a seat in the waiting room. Kate sat down, but reality must have hit her as she just slipped off the seat onto the ground.

When she came round, she was lying on a bed in the outpatients' department and a nurse and a doctor were looking down at her. They asked her name. When she told them, the doctor said, "Kate, you fainted, though it's not surprising with the shock you had. We have put a temporary dressing on that wound. We will be taking you to get it stitched shortly, so just try and rest."

Kate asked, "What about John?" and she started to cry.

"Kate," he said, "your husband is very ill. He has been shot through his lung and he has another bullet lodged behind his left knee. He is in a lot of pain, so we have him heavily sedated, and he is being prepared for surgery as we speak. Now you can do nothing to help him at the minute, so I suggest you get yourself a bit of rest. I will get your arm sorted soon. By the way, the police will probably come to talk to you as we have to inform them when someone comes in with gunshot wounds."

At that, the man who drove Kate to the hospital came in to give her the car keys, telling her he had parked her car in the car park as he had arranged to get picked up. He was anxious to know how John was. When Kate told him, he said he hoped he would be all right. Kate told him that but for his quick action John would probably have died, and she said she didn't even know his name. He said he was John Carter from Haverstown.

He said he had known John's mother for years. He said he would bring the unfortunate news to John's family when he got home. He left, telling her everything would be all right.

She must have fallen asleep as she woke to hear someone saying, "Excuse me, excuse me." She woke to find two policemen at the side of the bed. "Sorry to wake you," one of them said. "We are here to find out about this incident you and your husband were involved in with the British Army. What is your name?" the taller fellow asked. She told him. "Now, Kate. We know that you are in a state of shock, so we will take it easy. You just relate all that happened to you and your husband to myself, and my colleague will take note of it."

Kate told them how they had been there on holiday and were heading to the airport to catch a plane home. They came up to the checkpoint and she was asked for her licence, which she showed. She thought she would be allowed to continue, but the soldier went around to the passenger side of the car and mistook John for his brother Tommy. She told them that when John pointed out that he was indeed John, the soldier pulled him out of the car and pushed him to the ground. She told him how the soldier grabbed him by the throat and shouted that his four mates had been blown up and he was kicking John on the ground. She ran around to help John, who managed to show him his licence and how the soldier screamed at them to get the hell out of there.

She went on to explain how they had only travelled a short distance when she heard some sort of a noise and how John had slumped into the footwell of the car. She felt a sharp pain in her arm.

"How did you get here?" the policeman asked. She explained that a man pulled up when he saw her on the road, and when he saw how badly injured John was, he decided to drive them straight to the hospital and she said how glad she was that he did. "Who is this man?" the policeman asked. Kate explained that she had never met him before. She said he told her he was John Carter from Haverstown.

"Where is the car now?" the policeman inquired. Kate told him the man told her he had parked it in the car park, but she didn't know where. He asked her if she had got the keys. She handed them to him, but told him they had a lot of their belongings in the car. The policeman explained that they would be taking the car for forensic tests and whatever belongings were in it would be examined and kept at the Barracks until the police were finished with it. "We will also want to talk to John Carter," the policeman added.

"Now, Kate, I need your full address," the policeman said. She gave her address to the policeman. He then asked her if she had ever had any trouble with the Army on any of her other visits. He was totally surprised when she told him she never was in Ireland before. The police told her they would be in touch when they completed their investigation. They told her they hoped John would make a full recovery.

As they were leaving, the second policeman turned to her and asked her, "Have you seen Tommy Grugan about?"

"No," she said, thinking how sneaky he was to slip that question in at such a time.

She must have dozed off again, because the next thing she knew she was awoken by an orderly who tapped her on the shoulder, telling her he was there to take her to get the wound on her arm stitched. He told her to take her time getting out of the bed as he would wheel her there in the wheelchair. As they were going down the corridor, she asked him if he had heard anything about her husband. He explained to her that he didn't work in that department, but said, "I'm sure when they are finished working on him, they will give you a full report on how he's doing." He turned into a room on the right and there was a nurse and a doctor waiting there. The nurse helped her out of the chair and onto a bed.

The doctor looked at her and said, "Hello, Kate, from what I hear you were a very lucky woman today. I believe your husband wasn't as lucky."

"Please tell me he is going to be all right." Kate started crying. "The worst thing is not knowing."

"Look, Kate," the doctor said, "pull yourself together till we get this wound stitched and I promise you I'll get someone to contact you with an update on your husband's condition."

Getting the stitches in was very sore but didn't take long, and just as she was finished the orderly came into the room and took her back to the ward. When she got back into the bed, he asked her if she would like a cup of tea or coffee. She said she would love a cup of tea. He was gone and back again in a few minutes with the tea and biscuits. She thanked him and she realised she hadn't eaten anything since that morning. As she drank the tea and ate two of the biscuits, her mind quickly drifted back to John. She started to cry and, unknown to her, she caught the eye of a nurse who came over to the edge of the bed and asked her if she was all right. She was sobbing and her crying got worse, and she blurted out that she needed to know how her husband was.

The nurse put her arm around Kate and comforted her. "Stop crying," she said to her. "I am going to make a phone call over to theatre and I'll get someone to come over and talk to you about your husband's condition. I'll be back in a few minutes." True to her word, she was back within a very short time. "Now, Kate, I was talking to Dr Whitten, and he is coming over to see you as soon as he gets a minute. So, lie back and rest. He shouldn't be long." The nurse left, taking the empty cup and saucer with her.

In a short time, a tall man entered the ward with the nurse. He was dressed in green scrubs and the nurse showed him to her bed. "Hello, Kate," he said. "Sorry I couldn't get to you sooner, but John was our priority, as you can understand. Now let me explain to you what the situation is at the minute. We removed the bullet from John's lung, which was a bit complicated. The bullet in his leg we took out, but it is badly infected. This worries us, but we will just have to see how things progress."

"Can I see him?" Kate asked.

"Kate, he is still under the effects of the anaesthetic, and I think it would be better if you left it till morning to visit him. I promise the minute he wakes up we will tell him you were asking for him. I know it's not the news you want to hear, but the better news I have for you is you are free to be discharged, so when Nurse fills out your forms you are free to go."

She told him she was very disappointed she couldn't see John until tomorrow. She thanked him for all he had done for him.

Just as he left, Kate noticed the nurse coming back into the ward with some other people following her. It was only when they entered the ward that she realised it was Meabh and Mary, her mother-in-law. She burst out crying. When they got to the bed, they were crying, too. They hugged each other and didn't speak.

When they regained their composure, Mary blurted out, "How's John? Please tell me he'll live."

Kate told them of his condition, and they were off crying again. She told them no one could see him till morning. "Kate, we would have been here earlier, only the Brits were raiding our house and they wouldn't let us leave," Meabh said. "They wouldn't even let us make a call to the hospital. They also lifted John Carter because when he was coming home, he took your two cases from your car. They said he was interfering with evidence. Well, we hid the cases over in Grennan's house so as them bastards wouldn't get them. They kept asking about Tommy. They said they were disappointed that they shot the wrong brother."

"If Tommy had been at home, they would have shot him on the spot," John's mother said.

At that, the nurse approached them. "Kate, if you were to fill in these few forms with me, you could go home with your people. I am sure you would rather be out of this place."

It only took a few minutes to complete the form. Kate thanked the nurse for her and everyone else's help in the hospital. She told her she'd ring in the morning to arrange a time to see John. It was only when she got up to leave that she realised she had no cardigan as it had been destroyed with blood. Meabh gave her hers and helped her to carefully get it over her wound.

They headed for home and Kate thought about John being left behind on his own in the hospital. When they came to the spot on the road where they were shot, she put her hands over her eyes and broke into tears. Kate pulled herself together just as Meabh pulled into the street.

Chapter 10

When they went into the house, Meabh put on the kettle and her mother helped Kate into the armchair and put her arms around her. "Kate, we are so sorry at what happened to you and John. Two people who wouldn't hurt a fly." The two of them held each other and cried. Meabh eased them apart, giving Kate a cup of tea. She also gave her mother one.

Meabh took her own tea and went and joined her mother on the settee. With tears in all their eyes, there wasn't a word spoken for a good while.

"What happened to the room door?" Kate asked.

Her mother-in-law sighed. "When the Brits came into the house, they thought that the door was locked, so they just kicked it in."

Meabh continued to explain that they kicked the door in and one of them put their hand over her mouth when they saw her in the bed. They were roaring and shouting, and little Seamus woke screaming. The fellow with his hand on her mouth wouldn't let her go to the baby.

"He didn't stop me from getting to the child," Meabh's mother said. "I just pushed him out of my road. I told him we were dealing with a little baby here and to get out of my way. When I got up to the kitchen with the child they were leaving, as they had already had the place ransacked."

"That dirty bastard tried to kiss me before he left the room," Meabh whimpered.

"Where is little Seamus now?" Kate asked.

Meabh told her how Jenna had taken the day off work to mind him to let them go to the hospital. "And what about Tommy?" Kate asked.

"Tommy hasn't been about," Meabh added. "He wouldn't stand a chance with these boys."

At that, they heard a car pulling into the yard. Kate got all tensed up. Her mother-in-law went over to the window. "Kate," she said, "it's only Jenna with the baby."

Meabh went over and opened the door. When Jenna came in, Meabh went over and took the baby off her, hugging him tightly. Meabh's mother went over and kissed the baby on the cheek. "You wee devil, you survived your first raid by the Brits." Even Kate smiled. Jenna went over to Kate and put her arms around her.

"I am so sorry what happened to you and John, Kate. How is John?" Kate told her that she wouldn't know rightly how he was until she went to see him in the morning.

Jenna said she had been talking to Tommy earlier on in her house. She said he might try and slip home. Just at that, Mary went over to Kate. "I think you should be thinking of going to bed, my dear. But hold on," she said. She went out to the kitchen and a short time later she came back with a large hot whiskey. "Get that down you, Kate, it will make you sleep." Kate reluctantly took the drink and started to sip it. Meabh said she was going to ring Paul to see how things were at home.

Just at that, the back door opened and Tommy landed in. His mother got a shock when she saw him. "Tommy," she said, "what has taken you back here and all that's going on?"

"Don't worry, Ma, I was close by, and I decided to give you a wee call. I won't be about too long. A wee cup of tea wouldn't go amiss. Kate, how are you; or more importantly, how is John?"

Kate told him about John's injuries, and she started to cry. "Will I ever see him again?"

Tommy put his arm around her. "It'll be all right, Kate. John's made of tough stuff."

"Yes, but I can't figure out why they shot us when John identified himself," Kate continued. "I didn't believe you all when you told me that things like this happen around here. We were absolutely no danger to them." Tommy said nothing, but thought to himself that Kate wouldn't have talked like this a week ago.

At that, Meabh came back into the room. "Poor Paul," she said. "He is really worried about Kate and John getting shot. He was really annoyed. He said he didn't mind if I stayed here for a while until things are sorted out. I'll stay another week to see how things are. I think he's missing the baby, as he asked about him three or four times."

"You married a mighty man, Meabh," her mother said.

When a car pulled up outside, Tommy said that was his cue to go. He said his goodbyes and told them he'd be back. "Kate, tell John I was asking for him, won't you?" He was gone out the door.

Chapter 11

The next morning, Kate was mad to go to the
hospital to see John. Meabh said if Ma would
mind the child, she would take her there. Meabh
rang the hospital to see if it would be possible to
see John. She was told they could have a short
visit, but it would be short. They set off for the
hospital. Kate said her arm was really sore and
stiff, but she didn't want John to know she was in
pain.

When they reached the hospital, they went to
the reception, where they were told John had a
good night's sleep. The nurse said if they took a
seat, she would take them to see him. After a short
time, she came back to the waiting room and asked
them to follow her. As they were going down the
corridor, she pointed out to them not to be
disappointed if he couldn't talk to them as he was
a bit groggy, and his speech was still a bit slurred.
But she said that would clear up in a day or two.
She also asked them if they would curtail their
visit to a short time as his mind wouldn't be up to
a long conversation. At that, she stopped and

opened the door of the ward. "Now, John," she said, "two visitors to see you."

Kate rushed in past her and threw her arms around John. She was crying. Meabh felt like crying, too. "How are you, John?" Kate asked. "How are you?" She was crying even more now. Meabh asked him how he felt. He just raised his right hand a little. Kate kissed him again and again. He indicated that he wanted a drink of water. Kate took a jug of water that was on the locker and filled some into a beaker. She gently lifted his head off the pillow, allowing him to drink the water. He seemed fairly thirsty as he emptied the beaker. All this time, Kate's tears were streaming down her face. John lifted his hand and put it on Kate's arm. She kissed him on the cheek. John made no attempt to speak and drifted off to sleep. Kate kissed him on the forehead and, still crying, turned to Meabh. "I think we'll go, Meabh, and leave him to sleep."

She was crying going up the corridor. She stopped and put her head against the wall. "If someone would only tell me what's going on." She was crying so hard.

Meabh put her arms around her. "Kate, come on, try and pull yourself together and we'll go and find someone to talk to you about John. I wouldn't pass too much remarks how he looks there now as the nurse did tell us he was still suffering from the effects of the anaesthetic."

Meabh took her by the hand, and they headed for the reception. When they arrived, there were two women sitting at a table. "Excuse me," Meabh said, "this lady would like to talk to someone about her husband, John Grugan. He is in Ward 15."

One of the women started tapping on her computer. "That is Dr Whitten's patient. If you take a seat over there, I'll see if he is available." She went to the back of the office to use the phone, but they couldn't hear what she was saying. After a few minutes, she came back to the counter. "You are in luck. Mr Whitten was in early for an emergency operation. He said if you go to his office, he will see you now. Go down this corridor here," she said, pointing to the left of reception. "You will see his name on the door. It's about ten doors down. Okay." Meabh thanked her and they headed down the corridor.

They kept going until, sure enough, they came to his office. Kate had gone strangely quiet. She still had a hold of Meabh's hand. Meabh rapped the door. The same man who had spoken to her in the ward yesterday opened the door. "Mrs Grugan, come in and take a seat, ladies," he said. He went over to his desk and came back with a file which he opened and put on his desk.

"Mrs Grugan, the situation with your husband is as such. We repaired his lung, which went according to plan. Now it will take a while to recover, but we are hopeful enough he will make a full recovery from that.

"It is the wound at the back of his knee that is worrying us. For some reason, when we operated on it, it had become very badly infected. We are treating it with very strong antibiotics. I must admit we expected a better response to them than we are getting, but we will persevere to see what happens. Now you probably were shocked when you saw him.

"Well, he didn't respond to the anaesthetic too well and he is still very groggy, but I wouldn't worry about that. He also had a bit of a high temperature, but it seems to be coming under control. Have you any questions?"

Kate shook her head. Meabh thanked the doctor for his time. He walked them to the door and told them not to be afraid to contact him any time

On the way back to the car, Kate asked Meabh if she would take her into the town as she wanted to get John new pyjamas and slippers. Meabh told her that she was taking her home to rest and herself and her mother would go into town and get all she wanted for John.

When they got home, Mary was waiting at the door with the child in her arms.

Straight away, she enquired about John. Kate filled her in, telling her exactly what the surgeon told them.

She started to cry. Meabh took the child off her. "Ma," she said, "John will be all right. Now gather yourself together. I'm going to give this wee man a bottle. When I get him asleep, Kate is going to mind him and we are going into town to get a few things for John."

It took half an hour before they were ready to go. Kate was happy to mind the baby. She gave them a list of things she wanted and a few pounds, and off they went. When they were heading in the road, Meabh told her mother that she thought Kate needed a bit of a rest as she wasn't in great form. She also said they would be back home before the baby wakens so she would have no hassle there. Her mother said she was worried about John. She didn't like the news about his leg. Meabh said she thought it was a bit early to be worrying.

Chapter 12

Tommy waited for the nine o'clock news. He had been at the meeting the night before and knew what was coming, but he needed to hear it for himself. It was the main item on the news:

"Oglaigh na Éireann has being engaged in a ceasefire with the British authorities since last November. We have strived to stick rigidly to the terms of the ceasefire, but due to the constant harassment of the civilian population and the shooting of unarmed innocent civilians, we realise that the British authorities have no intention of keeping their end of the agreement. So, with great regret and reluctance, I must announce that we are pulling out of the agreement. Signed: P. O'Neill."

Tommy thought back to the meeting the night before. How some of the people didn't want to pull out of the ceasefire, while others were adamant the only way was to end the ceasefire. He felt some of the older war-weary ones maybe would be open to another bit of discussion before the final decision was taken. In the end the vote was taken, and they were where they were.

Tommy realised that things were going to be back like they were during the struggle. He thought he would go over home to see the folks as he wouldn't be able to get there as often when things kick off again. When he got home, he asked Kate how she was. She told him her arm was very sore and she would be glad to get the stitches removed.

"How is John?" he asked. She told him she had been in to see him again last night. She had given him his new pyjamas and he seemed to perk up when she helped him put them on. She said he seemed to be in better form and that put her in good form, too, until she went to see the doctor before she left. He said they were increasingly worried about the infection in his leg. He said they were using the strongest antibiotic, but the infection wasn't reacting to it. He said they were keeping a close eye on it, but if things didn't take a different direction soon, they would have to look at alternative measures. But he assured her that he would be discussing everything with her and John as they happened.

She said that was the bit that worried her.

Tommy assured her that John would be all right. At that, Tommy's mother came in the back door. She stared at Tommy with that look. "Tommy, I am after being down at the shop and everyone is saying that the IRA have pulled out of the ceasefire. Tell me, is it true?" Tommy told her it was.

Kate put her hands over her eyes. "Jesus Christ, what will happen now?"

Tommy told her the terms of the ceasefire and how the Brits were harassing and arresting people all over the country, which, according to the agreement, they weren't supposed to do. He told her that the shooting of her and John really put the whole thing in jeopardy. Meabh, hearing the conversation, came into the room. "Kate, what the Brits did to you and John was despicable; you two were no threat to anybody, and when they are questioned about it, they will deny it, just as they have done down through the years. I'm not surprised the IRA pulled out of the negotiations."

"Jesus Christ," Kate said, "I never could imagine myself and John being the cause of the breakdown of an international agreement. But I can understand your hatred of the army more now than before."

Tommy thought to himself, *This is some statement coming from Kate.*

Chapter 13

The next day, the phone rang. Meabh picked it up. She called Kate, telling her it was the hospital. Kate rushed to the phone. "Hello, hello," she said. She stayed silent. When the call ended, she put the phone down and started to cry. Meabh and her mother looked at her.

"What's up, Kate?" Mary asked her. Kate was sobbing at this stage.

"The surgeon who operated on John wants to talk to me." She fought back the tears. "There is a development with John's leg. They want to meet me at three o'clock today. They say they can't discuss it with me unless John is present. I know it's not good."

Meabh's mother put her arm around Kate and sat her down in the armchair. "Look, Kate, it might be nothing; don't be getting yourself in a state. Wait until you find out the problem." She was telling Kate this knowing well there must be something seriously wrong when the hospital rang.

"I'll make us a cup of tea, then we'll get ready, and I'll take you to the hospital," Meabh said.

As they were ready to go, Meabh reminded her mother to give wee Seamus his bottle at three o'clock. Her mother said that was the second time she told her that.

The whole way to the hospital, Kate kept wringing her hands and Meabh could see tears running down her cheeks. Meabh tried to pacify her, but to no avail. When they got to the hospital entrance, Kate gave an enormous sigh. "God knows what we're going to meet here."

Meabh got parked and Kate asked her to accompany her into the hospital. A quick glance at her watch showed it was ten to three. Perfect timing, Meabh thought. When they got to the reception, Kate said that she had a meeting with Dr Whitten. The nurse explained to Kate that they should continue on up to John's ward as the meeting would be at John's bedside. When they got to the ward, Meabh said she'd wait outside.

Kate rushed over and hugged John. "What is wrong, Kate, why are you here, what is going on?" asked John.

"I'm not sure, John," she answered. "Dr Whitten rang this morning to say he wanted to see me at three o'clock. He said there was a development with your leg."

John told her that they had checked it that morning and the nurse seemed worried, but neither she nor the doctor said anything.

At that, Kate saw Dr Whitten and a nurse coming into the ward. "Mrs Grugan, how are you? I'm glad you are here," said the doctor.

The nurse started to close the curtains around the bed. Dr Whitten started to talk. "We looked at John's leg this morning and we didn't like what we saw. As you know, we were treating the wound with very strong antibiotics, but we failed to kill the infection. Now brace yourselves for the next bit. The wound has turned gangrenous, and we are looking at an amputation."

Kate felt weak and the nurse put her arm around her. John put his hands over his face and started to cry. When Kate saw this, she also started to cry. Dr Whitten started talking again. "The better news is that we will do the amputation below the knee, which isn't as severe as losing the complete limb. The current situation means that we are going to have to do the amputation this evening before the infection spreads any more."

Kate was still crying bitterly. John hadn't said a word. Dr Whitten said he was leaving. "Take a while to yourselves. The nurse will organise some tea."

"Can John's sister come in?" Kate asked.

"Of course," the nurse said. "I'll send her in on my way out."

When Meabh came in, Kate was still sobbing. "John is going to lose his leg from the knee down," she said.

Meabh couldn't believe her ears. She, too, burst out crying. John hadn't said a word since he got the bad news. Meabh went over and put her arms around him. "I am very sorry for you, John," she said. "If there's one person who doesn't deserve this, it's you."

John just put his hands on his forehead and stared up at the ceiling. The girls dried their eyes and sat beside him in silence.

After a while, the nurse came back with tea and biscuits. She poured two cups out for Meabh and Kate. "I can't give you any, John," she said, "as you have to fast for your operation. Sorry." John didn't even take his gaze off the ceiling.

They sat for about an hour with little being said. At that, two nurses came and explained that they had to prep John for his operation. Kate and Meabh both hugged John and said they would be back in the morning. They waved to him as they left the ward. He never moved. Meabh was thinking how she was going to break the news to her mother

Chapter 14

When they pulled into the yard, Meabh could see her mother looking out through the window with the child in her arms. She felt a lump in her throat. *How am I going to tell her the bad news? She had been so happy that John and Kate came home on holiday, and now this.*

Meabh was first into the house. She took the baby off her ma and put him in the bouncer.

When her mother saw Kate crying, she asked what was wrong. Meabh said, "Ma, sit down." After a long pause, Meabh gathered up courage. "Things aren't good. John is losing his leg from the knee down."

Her ma let out a scream. "Jesus Christ, no, no. First them bastards kill my husband, and now they cripple my son. Oh, Jesus Christ. Why did this have to happen?" She put her head in her hands and cried bitterly. Kate became worse when she saw her mother-in-law crying. The baby stirred in the bouncer and Meabh said she would get him a bottle.

While she was preparing the bottle, Meabh also made some tea for her, Ma and Kate and brought it into them. At this stage, they had both stopped crying and Meabh wasn't sure if the silence was any better than the crying. It was time to put the baby down for a sleep, and with that taken care of, Meabh returned to the kitchen. Her Ma was the first to speak. "This will destroy John for the rest of his life. How will he ever be fit to work again?"

"How will he ever walk again?" Kate said, and started crying again. Meabh's mother went over to comfort her, telling her something would be worked out. Meabh said she was going to try and contact Tommy on the phone.

She came back into the room shortly after, saying she had got hold of Jenna and she and Tommy were coming over if the coast was clear. Neither of them could believe what was happening. She said she wanted to phone Paul and tell him the bad news about John and see how things were at home. When she came back into the room, she told them how Paul had been totally shocked at what was happening to John. He said he just couldn't believe it. He had told her he was missing her, but there was no hurry on her coming home if she was needed where she was. Just at that moment, Jenna and Tommy came in the door.

Tommy went straight to Kate. "Jesus, Kate, I'm so sorry for John and yourself. A man who hadn't a political bone in his body. These bastards don't care who they hurt; but by Jesus, they'll pay for this one way or another. We'll see who can inflict the most damage."

"Stop it!" Jenna butted in. "Tommy, stop it now. It's not the right time or place."

"I can see where you are coming from, Tommy," Kate said. "I didn't understand the way things were here. We are being fed great stories in England about how the army were trying to keep the peace in Ireland and were risking their lives every day. They could easily have killed John or me. He told them who he was. But it didn't matter. They shot us anyway. My God, why?" She started crying again and Jenna went over to comfort her.

After a while, Tommy and Jenna got up to go. "Tell John we were asking for him and tell him I'll see how things are. I might even make it in to see him," Tommy added. At that, they left.

Kate had to get her stitches out in the morning and Meabh said they should be there for ten o'clock. They headed off in good time and Kate wondered maybe they might get a sneaky visit in to see John. "Ah," said Meabh, "we'll chance our arm."

When they went to reception, they were told to proceed to Accident and Emergency. It didn't take long to get her stitches removed and the nurse said that she was really happy how the wound had healed.

When they were heading back to reception, Meabh thought they should try and get in to see John. "Come on, Kate, they can only refuse us."

"Excuse me," Meabh said to the lady behind reception. "Kate here has had stitches out in A and E, but her husband John Grugan has had his leg amputated last evening and we wondered could we get in to see him for a few minutes?"

"Oh, I'm very sorry to hear about your husband," the lady said. "Hold on, I'll check with the Ward Sister." After a few minutes on the phone, she said, "Yous are in luck. The Ward Sister is in good form," she said, smiling.

They took the escalator and when they got to the third floor the Ward Sister met them. "Your husband had a successful operation. The surgeon was very happy. But your husband seems very depressed, so I wanted to forewarn you. And I am asking you if you could curtail your visit so as not to annoy him too much."

When they went into the ward, John looked so down. Kate went straight over and gave him a big kiss on the cheek. He hardly moved. "Oh,

John," Kate said, "cheer up, cheer up for your own sake."

"Cheer fucking up? You haven't lost a fucking leg; you aren't going to be handicapped for the rest of your lives."

Kate was really taken back as John had never cursed at her before. "Look, John, I'm sorry. I was only trying to put you in better form, but obviously I said the wrong thing. I am very sorry. Maybe we should go and come back this evening at visiting time and you might be in better form." Once again John just stared at the ceiling.

Meabh took Kate by the arm, and they left the ward. There wasn't a word spoken until they got back to the car. "John never as much as said a cross word to me since we got married, Meabh," Kate said. "And you heard him yourself; this shooting has really changed him."

"Kate," Meabh said, "I feel very sorry for you. I know John's form. He's not like that at all. He is very depressed about losing the limb. But look, we will go back in to see him tonight and see how he is then. He might feel a bit better. Please don't say anything to anyone about this until we get it sorted out."

When they got back to the house, Meabh picked up little Seamus. Her Ma joked that she hoped the child wouldn't make strange as she thought the child was beginning to think that his granny was his mother as she had been minding him that often. Meabh laughed because she knew her Ma loved minding Seamus. The bit of banter took the spotlight off Kate, who was still very annoyed about what happened with John.

"How did you get on getting the stitches out, Kate?" her mother-in-law asked. Kate showed her the scar, saying the nurse told her she was very happy how she had healed. "I suppose you will be going in to see John tonight. I am worried how he might be doing. It's not easy to lose your limb."

"Kate and I will go in tonight," Meabh said, "and we can see how he is and, sure, if you want to go tomorrow night, Jenna will sit with Seamus." Kate looked at Meabh thinking, *If she only knew what went on at the hospital today.*

Chapter 15

That evening, Meabh and Kate left for the hospital, stopping at the shop to get a few things for John. When they went into the ward, Kate hesitantly went over to John to give him a kiss. He put his arms out and squeezed her so tight. They were both crying. Meabh said she'd leave them on their own, stepping into the corridor and closing the door behind her.

John apologised to Kate, saying he was totally out of order that morning. He said that he didn't know if it was the effect of all the drugs they pumped into him or that he was just in such bad form as his wound was terribly sore, but the nurse had given him another injection and it was more at ease now. Once again, he apologised. She told him she loved him, and she was so taken aback as he had never shouted at her before and it scared her. He asked her to call Meabh back in. Meabh came in and John put his arms out to her.

When she went over to him, he told her he was sorry he annoyed her that morning. He said he didn't know what came over him. They both told him to forget it and get himself better. Kate gave him the goodies they had bought in the shop, and he thanked them. He pulled back the cover and showed them where he had the operation. They were shocked when they saw the leg stopped at the knee. Kate pulled the cover back over and bit her lip to keep herself from crying.

"We'll get over this, Kate," John said. "The surgeon told me they can do great things with prosthetic legs. He told me of a friend of his who plays professional golf with a prosthetic leg."

He seemed in great form and Kate told him that she wouldn't see him tomorrow night as Meabh and her mother were coming in as his mother was mad to see him. They said their goodbyes and left for home.

Kate was in great form and was full of crack travelling back home. She said at least she could tell Mary that John was in great form. John's mum was delighted when she heard that John was doing well.

Meabh put the child to bed and shortly after Mary said she was having an early night. Meabh said that she was going to give Paul a ring to see how he was getting on. When she returned, she noticed Kate was staring at the TV but taking nothing in. There were tears in her eyes. Meabh went over and put her arm around her.

"Kate, I know why you are crying. You are crying with delight. It is great to see John back to himself emotionally at least." Kate smiled at her. "Do you know, Kate?" Meabh said. "I think a wee celebration wouldn't go amiss." She went over to her Ma's secret stash in the cupboard and took a bottle of vodka and a bottle of mineral and two glasses. Kate looked over and smiled.

The drink was poured, and the two girls settled into the two armchairs each side of the fire. Kate was saying how happy she was with John tonight. She couldn't get over how he had changed from that morning. He was even feeling positive about the future.

Meabh couldn't believe what Kate started to say. Kate told Meabh that she didn't want to come on holiday at all, but John was mad to see his family and friends. She said she was terrified when she landed in Ireland as they were only a couple of miles from the airport when they came to a checkpoint. They were waved on, but it scared the life out of her. Then, when Meabh's mother let her know about her dad and how she blamed the British Army for her father's death, she felt in a very hostile place. She said that John had told her about his dad dying, but he never put it in the same context as his mother did. She said that she wasn't sure about Tommy and his attitude to the Army when she came first, and how supportive Jenna was no matter what he did. Meabh explained to her how, when their dad died, Tommy didn't speak at all through the funeral, and when the Brits surrounded it to try and prevent a military funeral, Tommy just stood and stared at them. "John's a different person. He seemed to take the funeral in his stride," Meabh said. She went on to say that it really affected her, too, but she hadn't been brave enough to do anything about it. "When I was away and now married to Paul, it didn't seem to matter as much."

She explained why Jenna was so supportive of Tommy. When they were only starting to go out together, they were walking home one night when they came on a patrol. The soldiers started using terrible language to Jenna. Tommy told them to shut up. Three or four of them surrounded Tommy and beat the life out of him. When Jenna tried to stop them, one of the soldiers threw her to the ground and another kicked her in the face, fracturing her jaw. Luckily enough, some people coming along, came to their aid and got them off to hospital. "Tommy was in hospital for a week. Jenna was a long time recovering, and until this day suffers severe pain in her jaw in real cold weather.

"Tommy never forgot this, as you can hear from his talk. But Jenna, I still think she is more bitter about it." Meabh went on to explain to Kate that similar experiences had happened to a lot of young people around here, and that was why there was such a hatred of the British Army. With the effect of the alcohol, Meabh was really on a roll. With tears in her eyes, she blurted out, "What right had those bastards to shoot you and John? You are English and John wouldn't hurt a fucking mouse. They tell your people back in England they are over here keeping the peace, when they are terrorising the bloody people, putting them in prison and killing them. You have seen for yourself their attitude to you both, and then to let you through the checkpoint and try to kill you both. You could have been two corpses."

At that, Meabh got up and poured two more drinks for her and Kate. There was silence for a short time and then Kate started talking. "I didn't want to stay here at all when that explosion killed those four soldiers, and then there was that fellow in the pub telling me the English weren't welcome, and thankfully Tommy sorted that out. But what I can't figure out is why trained soldiers could not take our word on our identity when we had complete proof of who we were. Meabh, what really got to me was that when John was lying critically wounded, they never came to see if they could help. I couldn't believe how that man risked his life to get us to the hospital. He didn't even know us. He had never met us before. He saved John's life." She was crying. They were both crying.

"Kate," Meabh said, "that explosion you talked about was not the IRA. That was caused by people who didn't want the ceasefire. The IRA wouldn't break an agreement without announcing it beforehand."

Kate took a big sigh. "Meabh, I hate the British Army for what they have done to myself and John."

Meabh nearly fell out of the chair. This was the girl that didn't want to be in this country a week ago. Kate continued, "Your mother was right. The British Army were responsible for your dad's death. I didn't believe her when she said it at the time, and she was also right about them crippling John. I can clearly see now how she feels. I can't believe how much I've learned about this place in such a short time and how wrong I was when I disagreed with you all when you were telling me about the army. I should have known you were right, as you are great people. You tried to make me more than welcome, but it took a complete disaster for me to realise the real situation around here. Oh, I'm sorry, Meabh, for doubting your family." She started to cry again.

"Look, Kate," Meabh said, "how would you know any better? You were born and reared in England and only ever heard the English slant on the British Army's involvement in Ireland. Most English people who come here think the same."

At that, they could hear someone talking outside the window. "Shush," Meabh said. She went over nearer the window to listen. At that, there was a heavy knock on the door.

Meabh reluctantly went over and opened it. The door was pushed in, and she fell back against the wall. The soldiers burst in through the door. The soldier who seemed to be in charge spoke. "We have a warrant here to search this house."

One of the soldiers went to go into where the baby was sleeping. Kate jumped up and stood in front of him. "There's a baby asleep in this room and you are not going to wake him."

"And who are you, pretty face?" he smiled.

"You should know who I am. You or some of your so-called mates shot me and my husband at your bloody checkpoint the other day. That's who I am." She was staring straight into his face.

Meabh's mother had come out of her room. "What's all this about?" she said to the soldier in charge.

"We have a search warrant here to search this house."

"Well, let me tell you we have nothing to hide, but you are not going to wake that baby. It is bad enough to shoot two innocent people at that checkpoint, but coming to disturb people at this time of night…"

Meabh was following the other soldiers around as they were searching the other rooms. Kate started talking again. "I suppose all your people in England think you are heroes. Well, when I get back to England, I'll let them know what you are really like."

"Ssh, ssh, Kate," Mary said. "Don't get yourself annoyed; they aren't worth it." At that, the soldiers were ready to leave. With Kate's outburst, they seemed to have forgotten about the baby's room. As he was going out the door, the soldier in charge turned to Meabh and said, "Tell Tommy Grugan we'll get lucky one of these times." Meabh just slammed the door. When they left, Mary said she would have to have a cup of tea to settle her nerves.

Meabh said to her she had a better idea, and went to the cupboard and took out another glass.

Chapter 16

John had been making steady progress in the hospital and at this stage he was even feeling in a lot better form. The police had contacted Kate to say the hired car was free to be returned to her. She rang the hire company as it wasn't road worthy as the back window had been smashed from the shooting. They told her they would arrange to have it collected. She wondered what the situation about the damage to the car was. The hire company told her they would be making a claim against the Army, and they would wait to see how that materialised. She asked them what was the chance was of hiring another car and they told her that was no problem. She was happy with this outcome as Meabh was talking about going home in the next few days and she would be left with no transport.

The next couple of days proved to be a mixture of emotions. It was Tuesday evening and Meabh announced that she would have to go home on Thursday as the child had an appointment at Galway Hospital the next day.

Thursday was a long day. Meabh's mother nursed wee Seamus from the moment she got up. "What size will you be when I set eyes on you again, wee man?"

Meabh butted in, "Ma, don't be at that talk. When the weather picks up, I'll be up more often."

They had their dinner and Meabh said she would be better making a move as she would like to be home before dark. With her bits and pieces loaded into her car, she hugged her mother and Kate and headed off. Kate noticed the tears in her eyes, and when she looked at her mother-in-law, she could see she was crying, too.

"I hope she has a safe journey. I'll miss that wee lad," Mary said.

Kate put her arm around her to take her into the house, when a strange car pulled up at the gate. A tall man got out. "Is this Grugan's?" he asked.

"Yes," Mary answered. "What's wrong?"

"You hired a car," he replied.

"Oh," Kate said, "that's me."

"I just need you to sign a few forms and it's all yours."

Kate took him into the kitchen. He explained that there was a bit of expense from the car which the Army had taken, but as they were putting in a claim against the Army, they would wait to see how that materialised. There were a few days' expenses from when the car was first hired, but if she wanted to leave it until the final bill that would be all right. He got her to sign all the relevant forms and asked how her husband was. She told him how he had lost part of his leg, but he was making a good recovery. He wished them all the best and he was on his way.

That evening, Kate and Mary had just finished their tea. They got ready to go to the hospital to see John. Mary joked with Kate that she had never sat in a car with her before and she hoped she wasn't going to speed and put her in danger. Kate laughed and said the only fear she had was running into a checkpoint.

When they entered John's ward in the hospital, they stood in amazement. John was sitting at the side of the bed in a wheelchair. "My god," Kate said. "When did you get out of the bed?" She kissed him on the cheek.

His mother said, "God, John, I thought it would be a lot longer before you would be able to sit out on a wheelchair."

John explained that the physio came to him that morning and explained that in order to make sure he didn't get depressed and down of himself he was setting up a programme to get him mobile again.

He said he would start with him getting out to sit in the wheelchair. John said it was a very difficult task, but the physio and a nurse helped him to sit on the side of the bed. They showed him how to transfer himself from the bed to the chair.

"It must have been very difficult," his mother said.

"It was well worth the task just to be able to wheel myself over to the window to look out. I haven't seen a blue sky in ages. I was even able to eat my dinner at the table over there."

"Oh, John," Kate said, putting her arm around him. "This is just great to see you in this form. I thought you were lying down under your amputation, but this is brilliant news."

John smiled. "There's more news for you. The physio has told me that when I get fed up with this chair, in a couple of days he's going to give me two crutches and see how I can move, as he put it, on one leg."

"Jesus, John," his mother said, "I can't believe things are moving so fast for you." She threw her arms around him and kissed him on the forehead. "This is brilliant news."

Visiting time was nearly over. Kate said they had better go. Kate put a bag in John's locker. "There's fresh pyjamas and towels and a few wee treats for yourself, John, and we will be up after dinner tomorrow." She hugged him and his mother squeezed his hand. "We better go," Kate said.

John smiled. "Sure, maybe I'll leave yous to the ward door," he said, manoeuvring the wheelchair in front of them. They all smiled, and he waved to them as they headed down the corridor. Kate realised with all the good news she forgot to tell him about the new hired car.

Kate and Mary were both in great form on the way home, and all of a sudden as they rounded a bend in road they came on a line of soldiers walking along the road. As they turned to face the car, Kate thought they were going to stop her. She slowed down. She was worried. But just at that, the fellow at the back waved her on. She was so relieved.

When they pulled into the yard, Mary looked out the window. "Jesus, he's home," she whispered. Kate just stared at her. "Oh, sorry, Kate, when Tommy comes home when I'm not at home he puts the watering can sitting on the windowsill, so I won't get a fright when I go in. He thinks of everything."

Sure enough, when they went in, Tommy was sitting drinking tea by the fire. "There's tea in the pot," he said. Both women availed themselves of the opportunity. "How's John?" Tommy continued. "I thought I might get in to see him, but things are hectic, and I hadn't a minute."

Kate told him the great news they got tonight, and he was delighted. She then told him about the soldiers walking on the road and how they waved her on. He told her they weren't getting it all their own way as the Republican Movement were having great successes against them. At that, Mary said she was going to ring to see if Meabh got home all right.

"Kate, I probably shouldn't have mentioned the Republican Movement to you. Sorry," Tommy said.

"Tommy, don't apologise. When I came here, I didn't realise the real situation. I now look at John in that hospital and I see a different picture. Before your mother comes off the phone. I know she is going to bingo with Mary Gray on Friday night. I'll go and see John on Friday afternoon and I want to talk to you on your own if you are able to make it here."

At that, Mary came back into the room. "Meabh got home all right, thank God, and you would know in her voice that she's glad to be back. And what about you, Tommy?" she continued. "Haven't seen you or Jenna this couple of days."

At that, a car pulled into the yard. It was Jenna. When she came in, she asked about John.

Kate told her all about him sitting out in the wheelchair, and she said that was great news. Mary told her about Meabh getting home okay. They talked for a good while and then Tommy said to Jenna they should be off.

Chapter 17

Tommy couldn't figure out why Kate wanted to talk to him on Friday night or about what. Things had been very busy lately, and with rumblings of new peace negotiations and constant military operations going on, Tommy felt he didn't need any more problems to occupy his mind. But what was Kate wanting to talk to him about? The whole day he put different ideas through his head but couldn't come up with any; but sure not to worry, he'd find out Friday night.

On Friday, Kate went to see John on her own as Mary had gone to town with Mary Gray to do some shopping. When she entered John's ward, he was again sitting in the wheelchair. He looked tired. "Well, John, how are you today?" she asked.

"Very tired," he said, sighing.

"What has you so tired, John?"

"These here," he said, and he pointed to two crutches lying against the locker. Kate hadn't noticed them when she came in. "They had me practising to walk with those crutches all morning, and when I thought I had the hang of them, I kept going too long and ended up very tired. But at least I have to try and improve myself."

"Yes, John, but you mustn't do too much too soon, or you might set yourself back. But fair play to you for trying the way you are."

Kate told John she had a call from his boss to see how he was getting on and he said all of his workmates were asking for him. She told him she had spoken to her own supervisor the day before yesterday, and she was also asking about him. She told her to take off as long as it takes for John to get better. She explained to him about getting another hired car and how it had come in handy as Meabh had gone home.

John asked her how she was getting on with his mother. She said they were getting on very well, although they were missing Meabh since she went back. She told him Tommy and Jenna were there last night. She also said that Tommy was mad to come to see him, but thought it mightn't be safe with the permanent checkpoint across the road from the hospital entrance. John said he wouldn't leave her out to the door today as he was hardly fit to move. "Don't worry," he said. "I hope to soon walk to the car to go home with you."

She kissed him on the cheek and told him she would see him tomorrow night.

On the way home, she decided to go into Cafferty's chip shop and get her and Mary a fish and chip each. It would save Mary cooking as she would be only home from town, and she was going to bingo tonight. When she got to the house, she noticed Mary was coming from the coal shed with sticks and coal for the fire. "Ah well, Kate," she said. "As usual, me and Mary stayed too long in town. I have to get this fire lit and start the tea."

"Well, you can light the fire, but I have the tea home with me," Kate said. "How would fish and chips go down with you?" Mary gave her a puzzled look. "I know you like Cafferty's food, so I called in and got these," Kate said, holding up the bag.

"Here, to hell with lighting the fire," Mary said. "It can wait. Come on, we'll eat first."

You could see that Mary enjoyed the meal, and when she finished she made two cups of tea and went over and sat back on the couch, and Kate thought she looked so relaxed. "God, Kate, I enjoyed that, and I won't have to wash up. How was John?"

Kate told her about him starting to walk on the crutches and Mary said he seemed determined to get mobile again. Mary started to light the fire and Kate said she was going to have a shower.

When Kate returned to the kitchen, Mary had her good coat hanging on the back of the chair and her handbag and bingo board were sitting on the table. Mary said her lift would be coming soon. True to her word, there was a honk of a car horn outside. Mary said she was off, and Kate wished her good luck.

It struck Kate that since she came to Ireland this was the first time she was in this house on her own. She turned on the telly and was watching *Coronation Street*. Her peace didn't last too long. The back door opened, and Tommy appeared in the room. "Reporting for duty, sir," he laughed over at Kate. She smiled for a little, but then realised the serious stuff she was about to talk to Tommy about.

Kate couldn't find a way to start the conversation and there was real silence until Tommy broke the ice. "Kate," he said, "I came here tonight against all the odds, and I have been wondering all day what you wanted to say to me, and now you are saying nothing."

"Tommy," Kate said, "when I came over here with John, I had a completely different view of things around here. I thought the British Army was a peacekeeping force over here doing a great job, as most people in England think. I didn't realise what they are really like, but I have definitely learned my lesson this last couple of weeks.

"What has happened to John and to a lesser extent myself has really sparked something inside that I didn't think I had. Now I have something to say to you that might make you think I'm mad. But I have laid awake every night since John has been in hospital thinking how I could get revenge for what happened to him. I've turned totally against the British Army, and anything I can do to hurt them I damned well will." Tommy could hardly believe what he was hearing. "Now, Tommy," Kate continued, "I know that you won't confide in me about the Republican Movement. But I suspect that they must have some sort of help in England. Well, if you have help over there, I have work for them.

"In my job, as you probably know, I visit a good number of Territorial barracks all over England. Because of a lot of red tape during the week, I wait until Saturdays to collate the whole week's catering operation and there is absolutely no one there at the weekend as they are part-time and at home or else on manoeuvres, which keeps them away from the barracks. I could carry anything in or out of those places any weekend. I could have one of your people accompany me and if he was to leave something behind that was up to your people, but I stipulate I don't want anyone hurt."

Tommy couldn't believe what he had just heard. "Kate," he said, "I know that you have been highly traumatised by what has happened to you and John, but, Jesus, you don't have to go off the rails all together. Did you say this to anyone else?"

"Tommy, I am no fool. I arranged for us to be here alone so as no one else would know. I know you are thinking is this a trap or can I be trusted? I stood up to you people by supporting the Brits when I thought I was right when I came here first, and I can well stand up for myself and John now. Tommy, please take me seriously. Please."

Tommy's head was in a muddle. No one had ever come with this sort of conversation out of the blue before. He didn't know what to say. For once he was speechless. "Look, Tommy," Kate said, "I'm not surprised you are taken aback, and you probably want to talk to your own people about this, but, please, if you trust me at all and think this plan has any chance of working, please come back to me."

"Kate, you know you have taken me totally by surprise. I will have to put this round in my head, and as you rightly pointed out, I will have to talk to other people. But, Kate, don't say a word about this to anyone, and one way or the other I will come back to you. Now, I am going to head on as Ma will soon be home and it's best she doesn't know I was here talking to you."

. Even after Tommy and Jenna went to bed that night, he knew he would find it very hard to sleep. He thought about Kate and what she had been saying. Even when Jenna had gone to sleep, he couldn't bat an eyelid. Could he trust a woman who he only really got to know a couple of weeks ago?

Was she a trap set to catch him out? He didn't really think so, but he remembered Jim Black, who was set up by an informer and ended up doing eight years in jail. Could he even discuss this business with any of his colleagues? Would they think he was crazy? Jesus, he felt so mixed up. This was going around and around in his head, but he must have dozed off at some stage as the next thing he heard was Jenna getting ready to go to work. Before she left, she gave him a cup of tea, telling him to have a good day. How could one have a good day with all that was in his head?

As the day went on, his head became less muddled. He got in contact with Pat Dunne and asked him to meet him at Guiney's farm that evening. He knew Pat would listen to his story. They had both come through a long campaign together and trusted each other to the hilt. And anyway, a second opinion would be helpful. If his head was muddled over where Kate was coming from, Pat would see through it.

He got dropped off at Guiney's at seven thirty. Pat Dunne was already there. They went into the top room and Tommy related the story that Kate had told him. Pat listened intently. When the story was ended, Pat got off the chair, ran his hand through his hair, walking around the room a couple of times. Tommy couldn't stick it. "For fuck sake, Pat, if you think I'm a fool, just let me fucking know."

Pat sat down again, gesturing with his hands. "Tommy, you're no fucking fool. I've known you too long to know you are anything but a fool. But by Jesus, you have come up with one big conundrum here. Look, Tommy, can you give me time to think about all this and then we will have to sit down and discuss all this again before we decide whether or not to go to the big boys with it or not?"

Chapter 18

The whole topic was put on hold, as the next evening two young volunteers, Tom Cannon and Jim Kane, were coming away from an operation when they ran into an Army patrol. They abandoned their car and took off over the fields, but with the helicopter hovering overhead, they were flushed out from their hiding place after a couple of hours. There was no word of them since. Tommy was summoned to a meeting with Pat Dunne and John Mackin.

They discussed what went wrong and why they got caught. John Mackin said the operation had gone to plan until the two boys were heading back to base. The scout car cleared the road, but somehow, out of the blue, an Army patrol appeared, chasing behind the car. It seemed Tom Cannon put the boot down and got well ahead of them, but with the helicopter starting to hover, they decided to take to the fields, but they were discovered after a couple of hours. He went on to say Pat Cannon, Tom's father, had got talking to him after the Remand Court and he told him they got a terrible beating in the field when they caught them. He said they thought they were going to be shot.

John Mackin said it was a bit of very bad luck. He continued to say it didn't look as if there had been a breach of security. Tommy said the two boys would be a big loss as they were two brilliant volunteers, and it would be a big setback to the Republican Movement in the area.

There was so much security in the area for the next few days there was no one moving on the ground, and Tommy was staying well out of the way. All the time he was thinking about what might be going through Pat's head about what Kate was trying to plan across the water. Pat was a great strategist and would work out if her plans were viable, and if they weren't they could just dismiss them and send her on her way.

It was nearly a full week before Tommy got a message to meet Pat Dunne at the workmen's hut at Dawson's quarry on Monday evening. When Tommy reached the quarry, he could see the long tail shovel leaning against the hut beside the door. That was the clue to say that Pat was already inside, and the coast was clear. He parked his car behind the machinery in the big shed where Pat had already parked. As he approached the shed, he could see him looking out the window.

"All right, Tommy," Pat said as Tommy entered the shed. "Jesus, that was some week with all the security around."

"We are going to miss those two lads," Tommy answered. "They were the best two volunteers we had, and I hear the peace negotiations are going well again, but the Brits will see the capture of two top volunteers as a feather in their cap and might even pull back on their commitment to the negotiations. The only way we will ever get what we want in these negotiations is to keep the pressure on the Brits on all fronts, or they will see us as a weakness. We would want to be planning a spectacular sometime soon. But personally, I can't think of anything big enough to make any difference." There was a silence.

"A barracks in England," Pat said, bursting out laughing.

Tommy looked at him. "Are you fucking taking the piss? Are you fucking saying when I confided in you that it was all a joke?"

"Calm down, Tommy, calm down," Pat butted in. "I thought very carefully about all you told me that Kate was trying to plan. I think it is a very long shot indeed, but we have pulled some spectacular strokes in our time when we got together. But we always planned together. Now this is a long shot, but let's get our heads together in the next few weeks and see what we come up with."

"Jesus, Pat," Tommy said, "I thought you would think me mad when I told you this idea."

"Tommy," Pat said, "there's not many targets left in this country; the mainland could be the option. But don't think for one minute it will be at all easy if it ever happens."

Since Tom Cannon and Jim Kane were lifted, the Brits really stepped up their security in the area and everyone was finding it hard to carry out any operations. The Brits gloated on this at checkpoints and any time they arrested anyone. The leadership were becoming frustrated and were looking for alternative ways to break the hold that the Army had on them at the minute. It was after a meeting with them when Pat Dunne and Tommy were travelling home that Pat totally surprised Tommy. "Tommy, wasn't Grisly in very bad form tonight. You'd nearly think he felt defeated."

"He did seem down," Tommy answered.

"Well, what about taking another look at Kate's plan?"

Tommy was taken aback by the suddenness of the question. "I wondered where you were on that, Pat, as you hadn't come back to me."

"Tommy, I didn't come back as I hadn't completely thought it out, but after hearing Grisly and the other boys tonight it will take something spectacular to lift this campaign and put the pressure on the Brits. But, Tommy, sitting here in this car tonight isn't the place to talk about it. The two of us have to sit down and put our heads together to see how feasible the whole thing might be. Let's find a night that suits and take it from there." Pat pulled into the pub car park where Tommy's car was and said he would be in touch. Once again, Tommy's head was busted thinking how Kate's plan might work.

Pat Dunne rang Tommy the following Tuesday evening and invited him for a pint later on. He said he would be in Wheeler's around about nine. Tommy agreed to meet him at the pub. It would be quiet, and they could have a decent talk if they sat at one of the tables at the back of the bar. There were never too many customers mid-week.

Jenna dropped him off just before nine and he had just called a pint when Pat came in. "You may make that two," he told the barman. They took the drinks over to their usual table and sat down.

"Right," Pat said, "we'll throw this round in our heads and see if it's even feasible to waste time thinking about it. Now, Tommy, the first question I will put to you is. Do you trust Kate?"

"Pat," Tommy said, "I have put that question through my head a thousand times since Kate first told me her plan, and the only thing I can say is that when she first came home, she was totally against the Republican Movement, but since her and John got shot she has totally changed. I asked her not to say a word to anyone until I came back to her, and I am pretty sure she hasn't. Now, I don't know what you think, Pat, but I think I should be the only one to talk to her, and that way, if anything goes wrong, I am the only one she will know about."

Pat thought that was a good idea. He went up and got two more pints. He came back to the table and put down the two pints. "Jesus, Tommy, if we are to trust Kate and go ahead with this operation, we have some fucking planning to do. When do you intend to meet her again?"

"Well," Tommy said, "I'll have to go back to her soon or otherwise she'll think I don't trust her. I believe her idea is to accompany some person into the barracks and they would put the device in place."

"So that would mean the involvement of an English unit," Pat said, "and that would have to be sanctioned from headquarters. At least that means that the only contact that Kate would have would be with you and the person who actually places the device."

At that, the pub door opened and Jenna came in. She came over and sat down at the table. "Sorry to break up your conversation, boys, but dad was over looking at the cattle behind our house and he says there's soldiers lying in the ditches over by the old byre. They didn't bother him, and he didn't let on he saw them. But he is adamant they are on a mission, and he thinks that they are going to raid our house. He told me to get over and tell you."

"Jesus," Pat said, "your da is seldom wrong. The bastards never give up. Tommy, we'll have two more pints and I'll take you over to Uncle Johnny's and you can stay there for the night." He asked Jenna if she would take anything. She settled for a mineral water. With Jenna in the company now, there was no more talk about Kate's plan.

They drank the pints and headed out the door. Pat told Jenna he hoped that her da was wrong about the raid, telling her to stay calm. She went on home and Pat took Tommy to his uncle's house. He was delighted to see him as he always liked to help out as much as he could, and, as he didn't come under suspicion from the Army, he was a really good safe house, and as his wife had passed away last year, he enjoyed the bit of company. He went to the cupboard and produced a bottle of whiskey. They had a couple each and headed to bed. Tommy lay for a while with his thoughts flitting from Kate's plan to wondering if Jenna's house would be raided.

Chapter 19

When Tommy woke the next morning, he could hear Johnny up in the kitchen. When he reached the kitchen, Johnny had made a few slices of toast and he told him to help himself, and there was fresh tea in the pot. They were just sitting having a chat over breakfast when a car pulled up outside.

Johnny looked out. "It's Jenna," he said.

Tommy wondered why she wasn't at work. Then it dawned on him and he went to let her in. Straight away he knew she wasn't happy by the look on her face. "Well?" he said.

"My Da was right," she said. "They came at one o'clock and pulled the place apart. One of them lifted the harp that Brian Winters made for Da when he was inside and smashed it on the floor. Da called him a rotten English bastard and the soldier hit him in the face and he fell on the ground. I had to jump in front of him or he would have hit him again." Jenna was almost crying. "I think his nose is broken. Him and Ma are away to the hospital to get it checked. I rang work and

I told them the circumstances and they told me to take the day off."

"The English bastards," Johnny said. "Here, girl, sit down here," he added, pointing to the armchair, "and take this," handing her a cup of tea. "Do you take sugar?"

"No, thanks," Jenna said. "Just a wee drop of milk." Jenna looked at her boyfriend. "Tommy, I don't think you should stay at my place for a while. I don't think it would be safe."

"Sure, Jesus, Tommy, you can stay here if you have to; you took no hurt last night," Johnny said.

Tommy thanked Johnny, saying it would only be for a short while. Jenna said she'd have to go home and tidy up the place as it was an awful mess. Tommy said he'd go and help her.

The house was in a bad way, especially the bedrooms, where they had pulled everything apart. They worked away until it was almost back to normal. Tommy told Jenna he was very sorry for what happened last night and the fact that her Da had got assaulted. "My Da is made of strong stuff, as you well know," said Jenna. "The main thing is that they didn't get what they came looking for, Tommy. That was you."

Tommy gathered up a few bits of his own clothes and they decided to throw them over at Johnny's as Tommy would be staying there for a while. On the way, they stopped at the shop and Jenna went in to get a few bits of grocery, as Johnny wouldn't keep a great stock of grub, living on his own.

They decided then that they had better go over to Tommy's mother's, as by now she would have heard that Jenna's house had been raided, and she would think he was there and maybe had been arrested.

When they pulled up in the yard, Mary and Kate came straight out. "Oh, Jesus," Mary said, "I am praying all morning. How were you not arrested? Oh, Jesus, it's great to see you. I thought you were gone."

Tommy told them how they thought that they were going to raid Jenna's and he had moved to another house. He explained to his mother how the soldier hit Jenna's dad and how he had to go to the hospital.

"They had little to do to hit a man of his age," she said. "I hope he is all right."

At that, Jenna said she was going to go back to see if her mother and father were back from the hospital. Mary then asked Tommy if he was staying about, as she was going to make something to eat, and she would like him to join her. He smiled, saying he couldn't turn down the best cook in the country.

Mary went down to the kitchen to start cooking. "You were lucky you moved, Tommy," Kate said. "When we heard Jenna's was raided, we thought you were gone. I'm glad you are safe." Lowering her voice to a whisper, she said to Tommy, "My plan mustn't have gone down well with your friends."

"Kate," Tommy whispered back, "I'll be here on Friday night when Ma is at bingo. We'll talk then. Now, how is John?"

Kate told him how John was making great progress. How he was getting about very well on the crutches and how they were talking about him getting out. She told him the prosthetist had been to see him about his prosthetic limb. She said that the good thing was that John was in great form and was looking forward to getting back to as near normal as possible.

Shortly after, Ma came in to tell them their meal was ready. While they were eating, Ma said that her and Kate were going in to see John and she wouldn't mind if Tommy looked after the washing-up. He must have looked surprised, as Kate started laughing. When they were finished eating, they got ready and headed off. Tommy reluctantly took to the task that he was landed with.

To make matters worse, Jenna had come back and started laughing at Tommy's attempts to get the dishwasher working. "I'll buy you an apron," she laughed, turning the dial to the right position, and the machine went straight into motion. "Dad's home and thank god his nose isn't broken, but his face is black and blue with the bruising," Jenna said.

Chapter 20

That Friday night, knowing that his Ma went to
bingo at half seven, Tommy decided to go to talk
to Jenna at eight o'clock. As he went in the door,
he gave a shout to her so as not to alarm her. But
when he got to the sitting room, she was tucked
up in the armchair beside the fire, watching the
television. "I wondered what time you were
coming," she said.

He sat in the other armchair across the room.
"Now, Kate," he said, "I want you to listen
carefully. When you came to me with your story,
I was totally surprised at your change of mind
from when you first landed here. I put my head
around all you told me and realised with all that
happened to you and John you were genuine.
Now I have to tell you this before we talk any
more: if you were to set up me or anyone else,
you wouldn't be dealing with me. You would be
dealing with some very sinister people, and the
price you'd pay would probably be the death
penalty."

"I knew you didn't trust me," Kate said.

"No, no, Kate," Tommy butted in. "I have discussed this with some of my comrades and we think it's a runner and we have decided to go with it. But remember, Kate, like many other jobs we could spend months planning this, but if it's not going to be a success it won't happen, and we won't know that until the planning is final. Now don't mention this to anyone else other than myself."

Kate looked real cross at him. "Do you think I'm a fucking fool, Tommy? I want this to work more than you because when you didn't come back until now, I thought you didn't trust me, so I'm not going to sabotage it all by talking about it. It's in my head and that's where it will remain."

"Right, Kate," Tommy said. "I want you to explain to me in detail exactly what happens when you are working at these barracks."

Kate went on to say how her firm supplied ready-made dinners to the kitchens in these barracks. Her job was to get the orders each week, deliver the dinners on Mondays and Tuesdays and then collect the trays when they had been emptied. She went on to explain that she left the collection of the trays until Saturday as all the part-time soldiers were on manoeuvres and training, and as there was no one at all around she could get her work done faster. Sometimes, if she was under pressure, she would take a helper, and no one passed any remarks as she usually acquired the help herself.

"But hold on," Tommy said. "Places like this are covered in CCTV."

"No," Kate said. "This actual building is in Mackworth, and it is used as the store for the lunches. It is a building adjoining the barracks which is accessed by just a door in the gable. I know that there is no CCTV as some material was stolen from this area and it was said there were no cameras. I thought that they would have put cameras in, but it seems there was some problems with the owner of the building. And that was two years ago, Tommy. That is just the basics, and we would have to go through it with a fine-tooth comb as I want to get my own back on these bastards."

"Right, Kate," Tommy said. "I know that you are mad to get your own back on the Brits, but we have to think of your welfare and the welfare of whoever will accompany you. No point in two people languishing in jail for years, no matter how much damage we inflict on the Brits. I will go back to my friends and we will look at all the pros and cons, and as I said, if we see the slightest chance it will work, we will plan the detail."

Chapter 21

Kate and Mary had just finished breakfast when the phone rang. Mary stopped clearing the table and went out to the hall to answer the call. She came straight back in. "Kate, it's for you. It's the hospital."

Kate rushed to the phone. It wasn't long until she was back in the room. She was rubbing her eyes and crying.

"Mary, John's getting home. God, I shouldn't be crying, but I feel so emotional." Mary comforted her. "I'd better get some of his clothes ready. They said if I went in after two o' clock, he can go home."

"Jesus, this is great news," Mary said.

Kate spent the next hour gathering some of John's clothes, checking that everything was in order. A short while later, she set off for the hospital, with Mary watching her from the door.

When she got to John's ward, he was sitting on the edge of the bed and he gave her a big smile when she came in. "I hope you have my favourite shirt," he joked.

"If I was here as long as you are, John, I'd go home in my pyjamas," Kate said.

He got up on the crutches. "Carry that bag of clothes down to the bathroom and I'll change down there," he asked Kate.

They went to the bathroom, and she helped him get dressed. When they got back to the ward, one of the nurses was waiting for them. She asked them to follow her to the office and told them to sit down on the two chairs at the front of the desk. She sat down herself and opened John's file.

"Now, Kate," she said, "John has made great progress, but he has to be careful when he gets out. We don't want any setbacks. Now, while his leg has healed really well, it will be another few weeks before we can register him for a prosthetic limb. The problem we have is John wasn't sure if he could travel back to England with the crutches.

"We think he could, as he would get less-abled help at the airport. That would mean he could be registered in England for a prosthetic limb. So, we will give you both time to discuss whether you want to be registered here or in England. Now, we will not keep you any longer, John. I just want you to sign a couple of these forms and you can go. And here are your painkillers, but only take them if you really need them. Good luck to you both." John thanked her for the way everyone at the hospital had looked after him.

John and Kate went back to the ward to clear his locker, and all the nurses came over and hugged him. Kate thought she could see a tear in his eye as they went down in the lift.

Kate was glad she took his heavy coat as he really felt the cold as they made their way to the car.

She put his bag in the boot and then helped him to lower himself into the passenger seat. When they pulled into Mary's street, she came straight out of the house and ran over and opened the passenger door. "Great to see you, John. Great to have you home."

Kate went around to help John out of the car, and he got onto the crutches.

John and Mary walked into the house together and Kate followed with John's belongings. What a surprise they got. The table was completely set for a meal. "Now, John," Mary said. "You sit up here," ushering him to the chair at the top of the table. "You must be fed up with hospital food. I have made your favourite, Shepherd's Pie. Sit down there. Kate, come up here beside him."

John really enjoyed his meal and went over and sat on the couch while Kate and Mary cleared up. Kate asked John if he would like to lie down for a while, and he laughed and said if he never saw a bed again, he wouldn't care. Over the course of the evening a few neighbours called, and Mary was the nonstop teamaker.

The clock in the hall had just chimed seven o'clock when they heard another car pulling up in the yard. The door opened and Jenna and Tommy came in. Tommy went straight over to John and hugged him tightly. "Jesus, great to see you, John."

"Yes," Jenna said, "it's just great to have you home again."

Mary asked them if they wanted tea. Tommy and Jenna said no, and John said he was fed up drinking tea, but if there was a way in the world, he would drink a pint, but there was none of that in this house.

Tommy stared at Jenna. "Jenna, pull your car up tight to the door."

"No," said Mary, copping onto what Tommy was going to do.

"If a pint can't come to the man, then the man must go to the pint," Tommy said. "Jenna, get John those crutches. Here, John, put on that coat. Now come on, I'll help you to the car. Kate, you can get in the back with John. Ma, we will be back in a while."

When they went into Wheeler's all the customers gathered round John. They all wanted to wish him well. The barman stood them a free drink and before long the place was buzzing. Kate said to Jenna that she was worried that John might overdo it, but Jenna said she would make sure that Tommy wouldn't keep John out too long.

After a couple of hours, Jenna said to Tommy that it'd be better if they took John home. Herself and Kate took charge of John because they felt Tommy had one too many. And John burst into song on the way home.

When they got home, Mary demanded that John go to bed as she felt he was under the weather and didn't want him to fall. Jenna and Tommy left shortly afterwards. Kate went down to bed. As she cuddled in beside John, she thought how great it was to have him back home.

Chapter 22

Tommy and Pat Dunne, along with Grisly, were summoned to a meeting with the top men in the city. They were given the venue and the time, and they set off just after dark to avoid as little suspicion as possible. The meeting took place in a chamber underneath a flashy big pub. In order to enter it, there was a trapdoor and steps down to a big, spacious room.

Tommy felt it was very warm but was amazed at the size of it. A red-haired man with a beard seemed to be in charge as he beckoned them to sit down. The other two men with him were already seated and said nothing. The red-haired man approached Grisly. "Long time no see, my man. I believe you have a plan for me."

Grisly pointed at us. "These two men came to me with a plan a while back and I thought it was worth passing on to the leadership. Now I think our friend here is the best man to tell you it as it was put to him by a close friend."

Tommy wondered why he had put him on the spot, as Grisly usually liked to do his own talking. "Go ahead," he said, nodding at Tommy.

Tommy gathered his thoughts for a minute and started to relay how his brother and sister-in-law had been ambushed and shot and his English-born wife turned totally from being anti-Republican to wanting to seek revenge from the Brits on the mainland.

Straight away, one of the other three men piped up. "How can we trust an English woman that we've only known a short time?"

Tommy was taken aback by the suddenness of the question. To his surprise, Pat Dunne jumped up. "I have operated with this man since the Troubles began, and if he trusts her, she's fit to be trusted." He seemed surprised at himself as he sat back down just as quick.

Grisly interrupted at that stage. "These two men are top class operators and after plotting and planning with the lady in question, they think it is a runner." He went on to relate how she had access to this barracks as it was deserted at the weekend and that's when the action would take place. He told them that the plan was well checked by these two boys and the most important point was that there was no CCTV. He went on to say that in order to carry out this

152

operation, help would be needed from the boys in England.

The red-haired man stood up. "Right, men, listen up. Let's hear how you think this would work."

Grisly told Tommy to relate the story of how they intended to carry this out. Tommy went on to tell the three boys about his sister-in-law having the run of the barracks at the weekend and she had full access to the canteen and there were no people in or around it at the weekend and how there was no CCTV. He explained how she would need someone to take control of the operation and plant the device. But she was adamant that there should be no civilian casualties. The red-haired man quickly answered that no one wanted civilian casualties, but no one could guarantee that there wouldn't be any, saying that the Republican Movement tried to avoid them at all costs.

The three men went over to the far side of the room and had a discussion. They were talking too low for anyone to hear them. They must have talked for half an hour. When they returned, the red-haired man started talking. "Lads, we are going to look into all of this, and while I know you boys have studied it well, we will go through it all again.

153

"If we think it is a runner, it will probably be the Overseas operation who will look after it."

He went on to say that they would probably organise it their own way from their point of view. Contact would have to be made with this lady by the boys in England. He walked straight over to Tommy and Pat Dunne. He stared straight into their faces. "Do you boys think we can really trust this woman?" They both said they could. He said they'd be in touch and the three of them left. Grisly said they would wait fifteen minutes and then they'd go themselves.

Chapter 23

John was enjoying life getting about as best he could on his crutches. He would go for short walks up the road and was inundated with people stopping to talk. If he went for a pint at Wheeler's, everyone in the pub wanted to have a crack with him, and although he still had no interest in the political scene, he was a real hero in a lot of people's eyes because the Brits had shot him. The surgeon had contacted him to find out if he wanted to access his new limb in England or at home. The surgeon pointed out to him that if he chose England, he wouldn't have to travel home to Ireland every time he needed it to be looked at. In the end he chose England, as he knew Kate would have to return to work.

Kate agreed, as she knew she wouldn't be able to carry out her task if she wasn't close to her target.

Tommy couldn't discuss any plans with Kate on a Friday night now as John was there, and he would cop on to what they were planning. So, Tommy told Kate to let him know the next time she was going shopping on her own. She told him she had to go shopping for a present for his mother before they left. She said she would be in Duffy's clothes shop in the town before dinner tomorrow. He told her he'd meet her in Sparkles Café next door at twelve noon. She agreed to be there.

When she came into Sparkles, Tommy was already there and he had ordered tea and biscuits for them both. He produced a scrap of paper with a phone number on it. He told her to take it with her and memorise the number, but to get rid of the bit of paper when she had it in her head. "When you are back home and settled, ring this number at six o'clock on the dot any evening and just say 'Connie speaking'. You will be told an address and a time to go there, and stick rigidly to what you are told. That's if you still want to take part in this operation, Kate."

"Tommy, I watch John struggling to get around on a pair of crutches. I want revenge, Tommy, for myself and especially for him."

"Just remember, Kate, you are dealing with sinister people, but I know I can trust you."

They parted their ways, Kate telling Tommy they were booked to fly home on Sunday.

Friday evening, Mary was busy getting dinner. Kate thought she was rather early preparing it as it was only half four and she usually hadn't dinner until nearly six o'clock. Kate thought it was also unusual that she had her hair done today as her day for the hairdresser's was Saturday, when she spent half the day finding out the local gossip from the rest of her women neighbours.

Curiosity got the better of Kate. "You're early getting the hair done this week."

Mary paused for a minute. "Where's John?" she said, looking out the door. "Here, when he's not about, I'll tell you. The neighbours are having a farewell party for John tonight in Wheeler's. They have gathered a few pounds to help him along until he manages to get back to work. Please don't tell him."

"No way," Kate said. "But you think you would have told me earlier, and now I have to rush and get myself ready." At that, John came in the door. "John," Kate said, "you asked me to help you have a shower. Why don't we do it now before dinner and have it over with?"

John seemed relieved to comply and she thought at least he'll be ready for the party.

John was sorted and Kate sorted herself out and they had dinner. Around about eight o'clock, Tommy and Jenna called, saying they were going to take John for a pint. Kate asked Mary if she would like to join them. In keeping with the plan, Mary said she'd love to. Both of them got their coats and joined the others. They helped John into the passenger seat beside Tommy and the three ladies sat in the back. Tommy let John out right at the front door again like before to make it easier for him to get into the pub. They all stood with him until Tommy parked the car and then went in together.

As they entered, the lounge doors flew open and the cheer of the crowd was deafening. A massive, big poster hung on the back wall:

'JOHN IS OUR HERO.'

The tears rolled down Kate's cheeks. Mary grabbed Jenna and they hugged each other. Kate could see John and Tommy fighting back the tears. The cheering started to die down.

At that, Councillor Gerard Dunne got up on the stage and, taking up the microphone, he gestured to the crowd for silence. At that instance, you could hear a pin drop. After a short pause, he started talking.

"It is with great delight, and it makes me so proud to be asked to address such a large crowd who have come out to support a decent man with no political views whatsoever who the British Army decided to maim for the rest of his life. Not only that, and for good measure they also decided to shoot his wife. It is brilliant that both can join us here tonight, but remember, folks, these two people could easily have been in their graves.

"Think about it. The British Army do not care who they kill. We are only Irish Bastards in their eyes. But where John and Kate have no political orientation, there are plenty of brave people, both men and women, who are not afraid to take these thugs on with great success.

"We are still striving to resurrect the Peace Process and hopefully we will, as everyone wants peace; but not while these soldiers are looking down the barrel of the gun at us.

"Now, enough of that. I am asking all you people at the front of the stage to move and allow the great John Grugan to approach the stage."

John approached the stage to loud applause. Tommy accompanied him to make sure he didn't fall. Gerard Dunne came down to the front of the stage.

"John, these great people in this hall and also some who can't be here have taken up a sizeable collection to help you and your lovely wife until you get back to some sort of income. To come here and present you with this gift is easy for me to do, but those who deserve the praise for this are the people who organised this collection and especially the people who donated."

John indicated he wanted to speak, and he asked Gerard to hold the microphone for him while he balanced on the crutches.

"I stand here slightly embarrassed to think that you great people have thought enough of myself and Kate that you would put your hand in your pocket to make this great gesture. I will forever be indebted to you all. Myself and my wife were living a lovely normal life in England with some lovely people, but it seems to me the English have sent their worst bastards over here. But if they think they have scuppered my life, I will survive on one leg if I have to, and fuck the British Army."

At that, a mighty roar broke out. When it died down, Gerard said, "We can't leave Kate out. Come over here, Kate." She looked embarrassed. Gerard's wife Marian approached the stage with a large bouquet of flowers. Kate put her arm around her and gave her a big hug.

"Now," Gerard said, "the formalities are over. The idea now is for everyone to enjoy yourselves. Fulfil the task." There was great applause as Gerard left the stage.

When Kate rose the next day, Mary was already in the kitchen. She joined her at the table for a cup of tea and toast. "John's lying on this morning," Mary said. "Last night must have been a bit much for him."

"A bit much for us all," Kate said, knowing she often felt better in the morning.

"It was a brilliant gesture from our neighbours," Mary said. "Gerard Dunne told me they collected ten thousand pounds."

"What?" Kate shouted out loud. "Ten thousand pounds? Jesus Christ, that is too much. I just put it in my bag when John gave it to me. My God, you people are so good. Myself or John would never have expected this."

"We as a community look after each other. If someone needs help, the rest of us rally around," Mary said.

"Jesus Christ, and the things I thought about you all when I came here first," Kate answered.

"Kate, you didn't know anything about these people then, but you know now. Be happy with the money because if you were ever to try and claim compensation from the Brits, they will deny everything. They always do. You will be lucky if you get an apology."

At that, John appeared in the kitchen, looking the worst for wear. He sat down at the table and his mother gave him his tea.

"John, do you know how much money was collected on our behalf?" Kate asked.

"I don't know," John said. "I'll look when I drink this cup of tea."

"There's ten thousand pounds in that bag, John."

"What?" John said. "No, there's not!"

"There's every penny of it. Gerard Dunne told your mother last night."

"Jesus," John said, "that's too much. Why did the people go to so much bother?"

"The people round here don't half do things. That's just the way they are," Mary said.

Chapter 24

Saturday was a terrible day. Mary, conscious of the fact that John and Kate were leaving after dinner the next day, didn't feel in the mood for talking. John and Kate knew they were going to miss Mary, Tommy and Jenna. They had got on very well and due to all that happened they had become very close. Lunch was nearly eaten in silence, and afterwards Mary said that she was going into town with Molly Gray.

Kate was almost glad to hear this news as the atmosphere might improve and she could concentrate on packing their clothes. Mary returned home and Kate gave her the cardigan she had bought for her in Duffy's. Mary told her she shouldn't have got her anything, but she thought it was lovely and it would match a nice pair of trousers she had in the wardrobe. Tommy and Jenna arrived in the evening and after a while Tommy asked if they would like to go for a couple of pints. John seemed up for it, but Kate said she wouldn't bother as she was thinking about driving to the airport tomorrow. She said she would stay and have a crack with Mary on their last night. The other three set off, saying they wouldn't be very long.

Mary and Kate were enjoying a cup of tea and Mary was saying how much she enjoyed having her and John there. She said she was going to really miss them, and she told them that she hoped to have them back very soon. Kate laughed, saying, "Mary, I know I said I would never be back here when we came first, but I intend to be back soon, and I would hope to come here a lot more often. I love it here. I love the people. They are so good. I have never seen a community like them."

"Kate, the people around here have been welded together by the trouble bestowed upon them," Mary said. "When the British Army came here, they didn't care who they hurt. No one was safe from their viciousness. Man, woman or child. Why am I going on about this? No one knows better than yourself and John. Look at the way they targeted you two. Here, Kate, one wee drink will be well out of your system by morning." Mary smiled, going over to the cupboard and pouring two vodkas.

Kate and Mary talked away, and it wasn't long before the others landed back from the pub. John seemed in great form. He told Mary that he had thanked all the people in the pub for their generosity towards the collection. After a while, Jenna said she would have to go, and as she wouldn't see them in the morning, she threw her arms around Kate first and then John. Tommy said that he would be over to see them off in the morning, then he and Jenna left. John said he was tired and was going to bed. Kate said she'd join him.

They said goodnight to Mary.

Kate had hardly slept all night and when John woke around seven o'clock, they decided they would get up and prepare to get ready for their journey. Kate said to John that she would help with his shower and then she would have one herself. Later on, when they went into the kitchen, Mary was already there at the cooker. "Just a bit of a fry to keep you right for your journey," she said.

"Aw, Ma," John said. "There's no call for that."

Mary looked at him. "To tell you the truth, I didn't sleep all night and I thought I was better up doing something than thinking about you two going home." At that, the door opened. It was Tommy. "Never one to miss a good fry, Tommy," said Mary, putting more bacon on the pan.

Tommy laughed. "Wouldn't want to see good food going to waste."

Kate set the table and they all sat down to eat. After a while, when it was nearly time to leave, Tommy helped Kate to put their luggage in the car. Mary was hovering around, letting on to be busy and dreading the time coming.

Kate knew it was going to be painful for Mary. She went over and put her arms around her mother-in-law. "Mary, we hate every bit of this, but we have to go."

Mary was crying. John went over and put his arm around both of them, balancing with one crutch. They came apart and Tommy came over and threw his arms around Kate and John. "Mind yourselves on your journey."

Kate turned back to Mary. "Keep that room ready, Mary; we'll be back sooner than you think."

Mary smiled. Tommy accompanied them to the car, waving to them as they drove out the gate. Kate noticed that Mary had stayed in the house.

They had been driving only a short time when, to their amazement, they had come on an Army checkpoint. Kate could feel her leg tremble and she knew John was anxious as he hadn't said a word. There were three cars in front of them, and one by one each driver got out and opened their boot. A soldier checked the contents of each boot. As they came up to the soldier who was instructing the drivers to stop, he seemed to be distracted by a message on his radio, and to Kate's amazement, he waved them on. Kate held her breath until she was well clear of the checkpoint, remembering what happened when she and John were shot. John let out a deep sigh. "Let's hope that's the last of them we see."

When they got to the airport, Kate went to the car hire station to return the car and settle the outstanding account. There was a young man with a wheelchair to assist John to the plane. Kate struggled a bit with the bags, finding pushing the trolley a bit tough. She was glad when they had boarded the plane and they were taxi-ing out on the runway.

It didn't seem long until they were touching down on the other side. Once again, there was someone there with a wheelchair for John, and as Kate pushed the trolley, she was glad to see her Mum and Dad at the boarding gate. They threw their arms around each other when they came together. Her mother had tears in her eyes when she said to John, "Jesus, John, we are so sorry that this had to happen to you; and you, Kate, you didn't need this either."

Her dad took the trolley from her and headed for the car. "Come on," he said, "till we get you two something to eat."

Kate knew exactly where he was heading. He drove about ten miles down the road and pulled into Winston's Hotel, where he always went when he was coming from the airport. They all went in and ate their fill, and Kate's dad insisted on paying for the meal.

On reaching their house, Kate could see that her Dad had kept the grass cut and the hedges nicely trimmed, as it came into her mind that John might never be able to carry out this sort of work again, at least not for a good while. When they went inside the house, Kate's Mum made a cup of tea for them all. Kate explained to them how they were shot at the checkpoint and how the British Army were treating the people over in Ireland and how the people had helped them while they were there, and John told them how the community had collected ten thousand pounds for them. Kate's mother and father couldn't believe that the people had done this.

That evening, their neighbours and friends called to see how they were. Everyone was sympathising with them about what had happened. Some people just couldn't take it in when they saw John on the crutches and how much he was incapacitated. Some people couldn't believe how the British shot them for no reason. Most people were angry that such a thing could happen in a civilised society.

Chapter 25

It was later on that night, when everyone else had gone, that Kate's Uncle Godfrey and his wife April arrived. Godfrey had served in the Parachute Regiment and undertaken many tours of duty overseas, and now was a very wealthy man. He was actually Kate's godfather.

When Kate opened the door, he put his arms around her. "Good to see you home. Myself and April just came over to see how you and John are." They went inside to where John was sitting. "Ah, John," Godfrey said, "you poor devil you. You copped a stray bullet. How many times have I encountered this in my Army career? When you have idiots in communities who take up weapons against the might of the British Army, you will always have innocent victims. The Army must maintain control of these people, who even their own community probably don't agree with anyway." April nodded as he spoke, but she seldom commented in his presence, and sometimes one would think she was afraid to.

"Tell me exactly what happened, John," Godfrey added. John told him how they had mistaken him for his brother and when he proved who he was, they told him and Kate to continue on, and then they opened fire on them.

"Now, now, and why were they looking for your brother? There is something amiss here; they must have been spooked or something. They are going to knock the shit out of those IRA scumbags."

Kate couldn't have guessed what was about to happen. John struggled to get to his feet and faced Godfrey. "Listen here, Commandant Godfrey, Kate and myself were shot on purpose because your fucking Army are a shower of murdering bastards who are trampling over the Irish people, and your so-called IRA bastards are knocking the shite out of them, and all the community are behind them.

"So don't be going around telling your lying fucking stories about your great peace- keeping missions overseas, because any country the British went, they just slaughtered the natives. Now get fucking out of my house and don't come back." Kate was stuck to the ground. John slumped back into the chair. Godfrey and April had just let themselves out.

"Jesus, Kate, what have I done?" John said. "That cunt annoyed me. I couldn't hold it in any longer. He tried to say our shooting was an accident. I just couldn't take it anymore."

Kate went over to John and put her arms around him. She started to laugh. "I couldn't believe my ears. I never heard you curse as much since I married you. John, you told the truth, and when one tells the truth one can't be wrong. Godfrey, as my godfather, never gave me many presents, but he'll not be giving me any now." Kate pulled John closer. "John, you've never got stuff off your chest since you were shot, and I think you have just done that tonight."

She went on to empty the bags, thinking that when she gets her own revenge, things will be a lot sweeter.

Chapter 26

Kate returned to work the following week and received great support from her employers telling her if she needed any time off to assist John, they would facilitate her. John was well able to get about on the crutches now and she didn't have to worry about him as much. Her father came over and did anything that had to be done around the house that John wasn't able to do.

Driving home one evening, Kate realised that she hadn't checked the postbox yesterday, and when she parked the car she went over and opened it. She discovered four letters inside. Going in the back, she came on John struggling to cook the dinner. "Ah, John," she said, "I told you I would make the dinner when I came home."

John looked at her and said, "Kate, I can't just sit here all day doing nothing. I have to move about. If I sit around, I'll seize up. I wish I could get called in about my prosthetic limb."

Kate took over preparing the meal. "John, if you want to be doing something, why don't you set the table? That will be a handy enough job for you, and I'll have this ready very shortly." Kate hoped he would be happy enough doing that.

When they had eaten, they made two cups of tea and sat chatting. John asked how work had gone. He told Kate her mother and father had called around about three o'clock. They said they were just passing, but he told her he thought they were checking up on him. Kate told him a bit of company was no harm and anyway, he got on well with them.

Kate took the two cups and got up to start cleaning. As she cleared the dishes off the work top, she realised she hadn't opened the letters. The first one was the telephone bill, and the next one was the electricity bill. "My God," Kate said. "Two bills at the one time."

"What's wrong?" John asked. "Ah, the phone and electricity bills at the one time, but sure they just have to be paid."

She opened the third one, but it was only an advertising leaflet from a local furniture store in town. She reached over and lifted the last one. It was addressed to John. When she opened the letter, she was amazed to see the title. She couldn't believe what she was reading:

"Derby Surgical Hospital (Prosthetic Limbs Department).

John Grugan, your file has been transferred to us from your recent stay in hospital in Ireland. In order to assess your situation and the suitability of you to receive a prosthetic limb, we have arranged a date for you to attend our clinic. We can facilitate you on Monday 24th March at 11am. If this date doesn't suit you, would you please confirm tomorrow by ringing the number on the top right-hand corner of this page and we will arrange an alternative date."

Kate read it again. "John, at least we got some good news in the post." John didn't answer. She turned around to find he had left the room. She went down the hall, shouting, "John, where are you?"

John came out of the bedroom. "Ah, Kate, I am okay. You worry too much about me."

"You are more than all right. Read this." She handed him the letter and John read it.

He grabbed her and gave her a big kiss. "I am really excited. By God, I'll ring first thing in the morning."

John rang the hospital the next day to tell them the date suited him fine. They told him to be there at nine o'clock that morning and to bring a list of whatever medication he was on. John thought to himself: *it's two weeks, but at least the process has started.*

Chapter 27

John counted every day, but eventually Monday the 24th was here. Kate had taken the day off work to accompany him to the hospital. They left in good time and John was in great form. He never stopped talking to Kate about how he would be nearly back to normal when he received this prosthetic limb. He talked about how he might be able to go back to work, and he talked about so many other things that Kate was glad when they reached their destination.

When they entered the hospital, Kate told John to take a seat and she went over to reception to find out where they were supposed to go. When Kate showed the receptionist the letter they had received, she rang down to the Prosthetic Clinic and in a short time a nurse appeared. "John Grugan?" the nurse inquired.

John stood up and confirmed who he was. The nurse had a wheelchair with her and insisted that John use it as she said it was a good walk.

On the way, she asked John what happened to him, and when he explained, she reassured him that he was being treated by one of the best

Prosthetic Limb teams in Europe. She said they had great success with their patients. When they were almost there, she pointed to a blue door on the left. She told them that today's consultation would be held in there with the head of the team, Professor Garner. At that, she asked Kate to open the door and she pushed John right in.

A tall, red-haired man was sitting at a desk. "Mr and Mrs Grugan," the nurse said. She pushed John up to the desk and left.

Professor Garner came around the table and shook both their hands, saying he was pleased to meet them. He went back around the table and opened a file. "It was terrible what happened to you, John, but it's not our job to dwell on that. Our job is to mend the damage as best we can and as quick as we can. John, have you your list of medication with you?"

John took the list from his pocket and gave it to him. He studied it and wrote it into John's file.

"Now," he said, "I am just going to let you both know the procedure in this place." At that, he pressed a bell on the desk. "I want you to just lie up on the bed over here, John, and a nurse will be along in a minute to remove the dressing on your leg, and we will see what problems lie in front of us. Hopefully, not too many." At that, a nurse entered the room. "Nurse, I'd like you to remove John's dressing so I can have a look at his leg."

The nurse started removing the bandage, but when she came to where it was tight to the actual skin, she couldn't get it to come off. She went over to the cupboard and came back with a bottle of liquid. She put some on a rag and applied it to the bandage, which came off straight away, but John winced as the liquid burned into the wound, and it stung like hell.

The Professor went over and gently lifted the leg up a little and examined it closely. "Whoever did this job has done a very neat job. You can bandage it up again, nurse, please." He returned to the desk. Kate was feeling a bit queasy. She had never seen the leg without the bandage before. The nurse bandaged the wound up again and helped John back on to his crutches. "You can go back over to the Professor," she said. As she was heading to the door to leave, the Professor thanked her.

"Now, John," the Professor said, "we can admit you to the clinic next Monday. We would wish you to stay in the clinic with us until we have you mobile with your prosthetic limb. Our physio programme after the fitting is fairly intense and it is best you are with us all the time. It usually takes about a week. Sometimes a little longer, but in or around a week." He then asked

John if he had any questions. John said he hadn't, and the Professor said he'd see him next Monday.

On the way home, John said he couldn't believe things were happening so quickly. Kate said with all that had happened to him, he deserved all the good that could come his way.

Chapter 28

Kate found that the week flew as she put in a lot of extra hours at work because she had requested the Monday off so she could take John back to the clinic. John, on the other hand, felt the week dragged, as he was hanging about the house. They spent most of Sunday evening packing John's clothes, a few books and a few other items he wanted to have with him. His mother rang that evening to wish him all the best from all back in Ireland.

On Monday morning, once again, Kate set off in good time, and now being familiar with their journey, they parked in the disabled bay close to the door of the clinic to save John having to walk so far. When they went in, they were greeted by the same nurse who attended to John the week before. She got a wheelchair and once again wheeled John down the corridor, where there were a number of cubicles. She opened the door of number ten and told John this was where he would be staying for the week. She said nothing would be happening until around eleven o'clock.

Kate thought the cubicle was very nice. There was a telly and facilities for making tea; and looking out the window, there was a lovely view across the horizon. . Between them, they put John's clothes in the wardrobe and locker. They sat for a while talking, and then Kate put her arms around him for a big hug. "John, I really hope everything goes perfect for you; you are a brilliant man. I think I'll head home now. I'll not come back tonight, but I'll definitely be back tomorrow night."

She kissed him again and left.

Kate, being home on her own, started to think of the plan she had conjured up with Tommy. With John not around, she thought it might be a good time to ring the number she had memorised.

At six o'clock, she nervously lifted the phone. She took a big deep breath, put the phone to her ear and dialled the number. It rang half a dozen times and then a voice said, "Yes?"

Kate nervously answered, "This is Connie."

The answer came back, "Are you free tonight?"

"Yes," Kate answered.

"Go into town at eight o'clock. Park your car at Cavendish's store and proceed to 21 Balmor

Street. Go in the back gate and wait by the shed."
At that, the phone went dead.

Jesus, she thought, what have I let myself into? Oh, how she wished Tommy was here to guide her. She made herself a cup of tea and sat for a while, trying to get this whole thing right in her head.

After a short while, her mind drifted to think of John and why he was in the clinic, and she really wanted to get her own back on the people that had done this to him. She went for a shower, put on a change of clothes, and felt she was ready for her ordeal. She left the house at a quarter to eight and headed into town. She parked where she was instructed to, proceeded down Balmor Street, looking for number 21. On discovering it, she noticed all the curtains were drawn, with not a single light in the windows. Gingerly, she went into the back yard. It was very dark, and she walked slowly.

Suddenly, out of the blue, two people grabbed her by both arms and rushed her through the door. She almost fainted when they got inside. They were two very tall men with masks. They never spoke and they pushed her into a room where a woman was standing, also wearing a mask. "Don't miss anything," one man said to the woman.

The woman told her to take off her coat and shoes. "I have to search you from top to bottom." She searched her coat and shoes first and then she searched her from top to bottom. She even ran her fingers through her hair. *My God*, Kate thought, *Tommy did mention sinister people.*

The woman called the two men back into the room and she left. One of the men told Kate to sit on a chair at the table. They both sat down facing her. The man on the right started talking. "My father was from Co Fermanagh, and because of that I believe in the struggle against the British in Ireland; but you were born in England of English parents. Why do you want to engage in taking on the same people you grew up with?"

She related the whole story of her and John getting shot and how, when she was in Ireland, she realised that the people were persecuted by the Army, and basically, she wanted to get revenge for John and anyone else who had suffered at their hands.

The other man then spoke. "You have an uncle who served with the Parachute Regiment."

She was stumped for a second. How would he know that? Gathering her senses together, she explained that her uncle had served mostly overseas, and she never really knew him until he retired. She said he was her godfather, but it never really meant much to him. She said she would probably never have contact with him again, explaining the row that John had with him the night he came to visit. She said his attitude that night really turned her more against the British Army.

The first man then asked about her idea for this barracks in Barrow. She asked if the people back in Ireland had filled him in. He leaned forward towards her. "I want to hear it from you."

She was a little taken aback when he said this. So, she gathered herself together again and explained the whole operation just as she had told Tommy. They asked her a few questions on different aspects of the plan, and she tried to explain as best she could. The two men left the room and she felt very uneasy sitting there on her own.

They didn't come back for what she felt was ages. They didn't sit this time. They stood over her. She felt very intimidated by this. One man started talking. "We are going to give your plan complete consideration. We will go through it inch by inch. Give us a week and ring that number again and we will guide you from there."

Kate nervously said, "Can I ask a question?"

"Ask away, but we mightn't answer it."

"Could I ring you during office hours as my husband will be at home, and I don't want him to know what I am doing?"

"Ring at one o'clock. Now, before you go, if there is any breach in security on your behalf you will no doubt receive the death penalty. One of our people has taken the number of your car beyond at Cavendish's, so you will be easily traced."

One of the men left the room at that stage. The other man told her after a few minutes to leave the way she had come in as his mate had checked the coast was clear. He showed her to the outside door, and he closed it after her.

As she walked back to her car, her head was in a tizzy. She wondered about all she had just witnessed. It seemed like a dream. When she got home, she couldn't settle. She went over to the cupboard and poured herself a stiff drink and settled back into the couch. All sorts of thoughts went through her head about what had happened tonight. Once again, she wished Tommy was here to tell her what to do.

Then her mind switched to John. *Jesus, I wonder how he got on today?* She wouldn't see him until tomorrow night. *I can't wait*, she thought, heading off to bed. It took a while to sleep, but she eventually nodded off.

Chapter 29

The next day at work, nothing seemed to go right. Anything that could go wrong went wrong; so much so that she decided at dinner time to eat in the local restaurant. This would mean she could go in to visit John sooner as she wouldn't have to cook dinner when she went home. Fortunately, the second half of the day went a lot better.

When she eventually got home, she had a shower, changed her clothes and headed off to visit John. She stopped at a shop on the way to get him a few goodies. Having parked up, she made her way into the clinic. She was greeted inside by a nurse. "Mrs Grugan, how are you? John is in great form. You know he is in number ten. He'll be waiting for you."

At that, Kate headed down the corridor. When she came to John's cubicle, she opened the door slowly. John was lying on the bed, watching the television. He looked surprised when Kate came in.

She went over and kissed him, and he turned off the television and put the remote on the locker. He pulled himself around and sat on the edge of the bed. He grabbed her hands and looked into her face. "How are you, Kate?"

"I am okay, John. How are you? What happened today? Are there any developments?"

"Well, Kate, if there was one person examined that leg today, there was ten. They were doing all sorts of calculations and measurements. They all seemed to know what they were doing, and a couple of them were great crack."

Kate then realised that she hadn't given John his bag of goodies. When she put them on his lap, he opened up the bag. "Ah, my favourite pastry." He put the bag on the bed and reached for his crutches.

"What's up, John?" Kate asked.

"You bring me my favourite pastry and I'm not going to have a cup of tea with it. Will you join me?"

"John, of course I'll join you; but you stay where you are. I'll make the tea."

He told her to turn on the switch at the wall and that would give her hot water in the tea machine. He also told her she'd find the teabags and cutlery in the cupboard underneath. She'd find the milk in the fridge over by the door. Kate made the tea and took it back over to John. He took two pastries from the bag and offered one to

Kate. She said she just wanted a cup of tea. John put it back in the bag, joking that he didn't want to give it away anyway.

Kate asked John if he was bored being in here. He said he wasn't as the morning was taken up with the doctors coming and going. "Anyone who is mobile enough goes down to the Canteen/Recreation Room to dine, and when the doctors are finished up in the evening, they go back down again for the tea. The food is very good and some of the patients who are able can have a game of pool." He went on to say he couldn't play. He wished he could, as he would love a game of pool.

"Ah, never mind, John," Kate said. "The way things are going, it won't be long until you will be able."

John said he was sitting talking to a nice chap called Nigel. He said his injury was something similar to his own and he was almost ready to return home. He said this gave him great hope. They talked on for a good while and after some time Kate said she'd better go.

"I'm sorry you have to go home to an empty house," John said. "But here, I'll leave you to the outside door." He got his crutches and they walked slowly to the door. John kissed her and she headed out the door. When Kate was opening the car door, she looked back and John was still standing there looking after her.

The next day, Kate found work went an awful lot better. She was in better form herself as she was happy to see John had settled well at the clinic and enjoyed the visit last night.

She was on her last call in work, and she was glad to be getting home on time. When she got home, she made a bit of grub, got a change of clothes and she was on her way to see John again.

When she got to John's cubicle, she opened the door and was surprised to find him sitting talking to another man. When he saw Kate, he jumped up. "Kate, well, how are you? This is Nigel. Sorry, we got carried away in conversation and didn't realise the time."

Nigel shook hands with her, told John he'd catch up with him tomorrow and left.

"Sorry, Kate," John said. "I didn't realise it was visiting time."

"God," Kate said, "if I left you here much longer, you'd forget all about me altogether," letting on to be in bad form.

John came over and put his arms around her. "I am sorry, Kate."

Kate laughed at him. "I am only joking, John. Go and get your pastry and I'll make the tea."

John was relieved, and Kate went over and made the tea. They sat talking about how their day went.

John then went on to talk about Nigel. He told Kate that Nigel could almost walk perfectly with his prosthetic limb. He went on to say that he hoped he would recover as well as him.

"What happened to him in the first place?" Kate asked.

John hesitated for a second. "Kate, it's ironic what happened to him and that he ended up in here with me."

"What do you mean?" Kate asked.

"Kate, he was blown up in an IRA landmine in Ireland." Kate didn't know what to think. "Kate, he hated being in the British Army. He told me his parents were alcoholics and his father died when he was eight. His mother wasn't able to look after him and he was taken into care. When he was leaving school at sixteen, his social workers encouraged him to join the British Army. He told me when he was training, he was bullied because he had no one to stick up for him. He said when he joined his regiment the bullying continued as the top brass picked on the most vulnerable to humiliate in front of the other soldiers. He said even on patrol in Ireland he had seen fierce injustice being meted out to totally innocent people. When I told him what happened to us, he said he wasn't one bit surprised. He actually apologised to me as if he had done it himself."

Kate was taken aback. She didn't know what to think. There was no conversation for a minute.

"Kate," John said, "I know you have turned against the Army because of what happened to us, but when I heard what happened to Nigel, I didn't know what to think at first, but when he told me his whole life story, I did feel sorry for him. He hasn't even g o t anyone to visit him in here."

"John," Kate butted in, "I know you inside out and I know that you see the good side of everyone, and with the two of you in here together with the same injury you are bound to have a bond. It's evident from what you have told me that he is not the same type of person as those animals who shot us. Look, John, we shouldn't be worrying about all this. We have to get you out of here, so put all this behind you and let's get you back on the road."

They talked on for a good while and then Kate said it was time to go. John got the crutches and once again left her to the door. They kissed and she left for home.

When Kate reached home, she was thinking of what John had said about Nigel, and it proved a point that one could probably find a couple of decent soldiers, but the rest were the same as the ones who shot her and John. She went and got herself a night cap and thought for a good while about her plan for their revenge. She decided that she would make the phone call tomorrow.

Kate made sure to be back in her office by one o'clock. She checked about the store to see if anyone was about that might hear her. With the coast clear, on the dot of one o'clock she dialled the number. Once again, the phone rang a few times. Then a male voice answered.

"This is Connie, hello," Kate said.

"Took your time to come back. Are you free tonight?"

"No, but I can be free tomorrow night."

"Same place. Eight o'clock." At that, the line went dead.

When Kate got home that evening, she had a shower and made a bite to eat. Just as she was finishing her grub, the phone rang. It was her dad enquiring how John was. She told him how he was doing well and then it dawned on her. "Why don't you and Mum go and see him tomorrow night?" Her father thought this was a great idea.

They talked on a bit and when she came off the phone, she packed some clean clothes to bring into John. On her way there, she stopped off at the shop to get him some more goodies.

When she went into John's room, Nigel was there again, sitting talking to him. He greeted her and left. John was glad to see her and especially when she had the bag of goodies. She took some of his dirty clothes from the locker and put the fresh ones in their place. They talked away and John was telling her all that had happened to him during the day. She made the two of them a cup of tea and John rummaged in the bag until he found a packet of Jaffa Cakes. He gave her some and he was eating some himself. She told him that her mother and father were coming to see him tomorrow night and she thought she would give tomorrow night a miss herself. He told her that he thought that was a good idea as she must feel tired from working and coming to see him every night.

It was time to go, and once again John walked down to the door with her. She gave him a kiss and a hug and headed off.

When she got home, she started thinking about tomorrow night and how it might go, and she poured herself a nightcap to settle herself. Her head was in a muddle. She finished her drink and went to bed. For some reason, she was missing John very much tonight.

She wished he was home again. At least he won't be on his own tomorrow night, and Mum and Dad will have look after him . She pulled the blanket over her head, hoping sleep would come quickly.

The next day, Kate was awfully uneasy at work. She couldn't concentrate all day. She was glad to be finished and heading home from work. She just had a sandwich when she got home as she was in no mood for cooking, and she wasn't even sure she wanted to eat that much. She got cleaned up and sat down to settle her head to think what she would be asked about tonight.

The time had come to head off. She parked in the usual place. Checking that no one was watching her, she set off for the house. When she went into the yard, the back door opened and a tall man with a mask ushered her inside. Once again, she was searched in the room by a woman. She didn't know if it was the same woman as she again had a mask on. Like the last time, the woman left the room and one man came in. She wondered why there weren't two.

The man started talking. "Sorry about the searching, but we can't take any chances." He seemed a bit more friendly. "We have gone through this operation with a fine-tooth comb, and we think it will work. Now, the only one who can fuck this up is you. So, if you can keep your mouth shut and do exactly what you are told, everything will go all right. When are you going to that barracks again?" Kate answered she would be going on Saturday morning. "What time?" he asked.

"About ten o'clock," Kate said.

"Right. Do you know Chichester Road in Barrow?" he asked.

"Yes," replied Kate. "I travel that road because it is a shortcut to the barracks," Kate told him.

"Right, there is a phone box right beside that large Carpetright store on that road. There will be a man standing in that phone box. And if the phone box is occupied, he will be standing against the wall beside it. He will be wearing a red baseball cap and glasses.

"When you pull up at Carpetright, he will approach you and get into your van. What colour is your van?" Kate told him it was light blue and gave him the registration of it. "Okay," the man said. "This man will be called Clive. That's all you have to know. He will instruct you from then on." He stood up over her again. "I have warned you of the consequences if anything goes wrong. Now you can go." He let her out the door.

When she returned home, she made herself a cup of tea and sat down, wondering what position she had left herself in now. She thought of all the time that had lapsed since the shooting and was wondering if she would ever see the day when she would get satisfaction. Part of her was wondering, with the time lapse, was it a waste of time going ahead with this plan? But then something flashed into her head how much John had suffered and the pain he had gone through both physically and mentally. She quickly gathered herself together and realised she was going ahead with this plan. She felt every confidence in herself as she headed for bed.

When she finished work the next evening, she got ready to go in and see John. She made her usual stop at the shop and this time added in two choc ices as she fancied one herself and she knew John would be glad of one. When she went in the door of the clinic, she was surprised to see John standing in the foyer.

"John," she said, taken aback, "is there anything wrong?"

"No," said John. "I was watching the clock and I knew you would be along around now, so I just decided to come down and meet you." There was a funny grin on his face.

"What is wrong, John? Why are you grinning like that?" Kate asked.

John burst out laughing. "You haven't even noticed," he said. He went into a bigger fit of laughing.

"John, please tell me what's up," Kate said.

"I'm back on two feet," he replied. "One of them mightn't be my own, but it's fitting me well."

Kate looked down. How hadn't she noticed? John had his prosthetic leg fitted and she hadn't noticed. He was still on crutches, but it was progress. She threw her arms around him and kissed the face off him, and then she burst into tears on his shoulder.

"Come on, come on, Kate," John said. "Dry your eyes and we will go up to the room. I'll tell you about the whole procedure."

When they got to the room, Kate put the bag on the table and suddenly thought about the choc ices. "God, John, we'd better eat these before they melt." John was happy to get the choc ice.

They both sat down, and John proceeded to tell her all about the fitting of the prosthetic limb. He told her how they came yesterday to check the wound. They found it okay and said they were going to show him how to manage the fitting of the leg. They showed him how to always check the stump for redness or infection. If this happened, he was to get it treated right away. If everything was all right, they showed him how to place the liner and the sock on the stump in order to put the stump into the top of the prosthetic limb. They also told him to make sure to keep all material clean at all times.

He went on to tell her how they had him walking slowly holding on to parallel bars. They told him that at the start he should use the crutches until he was able to manage without them. They also recommended that he didn't wear the limb all the time until the stump got used to it. They told him not to wear it in the shower and to practice getting into and out of bed without the limb. He said the physio was working on this aspect with him. He also went on to tell her that this limb he had now was only a temporary one and when he was totally able to manage on his own he would get a new one.

Kate scratched her head. "A lot to take in, John," Kate said. "But I'll be able to help you in the shower," she joked. "How did you get on with Mum and Dad last night?"

"Great," John said.

Kate went over to see if there were any dirty clothes in the locker. She stood back in amazement. She lifted out the bottle of Baileys. "Where did this come from?" she asked.

John just laughed. "Your da knows how to visit the sick."

Kate just laughed. After a while, she headed for home. Tomorrow is the day.

Chapter 30

Kate got out of bed the next morning and while in the shower a strange sensation came over her. Here she was this morning going to meet some strange man that she knew nothing about. What if something went wrong? What would be the consequences if something went wrong? They had told her the price if she messed up. She stood there and just let the water flow down over her head and shoulders. Then something in her head told her: get out and get dressed and get the job done that has to be done.

The town clock was just striking ten when she was entering Barrow. She headed for Chichester Street in keeping with the plan. As she came close to Carpetright, she scanned the phone box and saw a figure inside. She looked closer as she passed it and sure enough the man with the red baseball cap and glasses was in place as had been arranged. She pulled up and parked right beside Carpetright. At this stage, Kate was very nervous. She watched the phone box in the wing mirror, but the person inside made no move to approach the van. *What is wrong? Does he not see me? Have they changed their mind? Oh, why did I ever get involved?* thought Kate.

Just at that, Kate looked over to the other side of the road. Her heart nearly jumped out of her chest. There were two policemen about to cross the street in her direction. *Jesus, what did I get my get myself into?* she asked herself. As the police got closer, she grabbed a heap of papers and let on she was checking through them. As they got up to the van, one policeman took a glance at the tax disc on the windscreen and they continued down the footpath, heading in the direction of the phone box. Kate watched them intently. As they were passing the phone box, the man had the phone up to his ear as if he was making a phone call. He had turned and faced away from them when they were passing. Kate could see at this stage that they had turned the corner into Buswell Street. They were out of sight at last. At that, the man left the phone box and was walking towards the van. Kate was still in a tizzy. The man opened the door and got in. "I'm Clive. Thought we were set up there," he laughed. "You know the plan. Let's go."

Kate thought he seemed nice enough and made her at ease. This would allow her to relax on the rest of the journey.

'Clive' never spoke again until they reached the barracks. "Winston Churchill Territorial Barracks. Jesus, I never thought I'd get inside one of these," he said.

Kate drove around to the back gate and let herself in. Clive got out of the van with her and said he would have a look around. When he came back, Kate was still loading the food containers into the van. She was surprised when he gave her a help with the last of them. Kate locked up and they were on their way home.

On the way home, Clive inquired of her if it was always as quiet there on a Saturday. She told him the same story she had told his friends in the house that night. He told her that his friends would be contacting her during the week. He asked her for her phone number, and he repeated it a few times to memorise it in his head, she thought. Kate told him to ring at dinner time as she was always in the office, and it would be the best time to get hold of her. He told her to leave him back at the phone box. She pulled into a parking space across the road and as he was getting out he said, "See you soon."

She headed on out the road. She decided to stop at Gresham's Café. She liked this place and she needed to sit down and clear her head. When the waitress brought her order, she sat back and for the first time that day she relaxed and enjoyed her break. She thought how uptight she had got when she saw the police, but Clive's attitude seemed to put her at ease. Of course, she thought to herself, the job isn't finished yet. She decided to put that to the back of her mind for now. She paid the bill and headed off to finish her day's work.

When Kate got home, she prepared something to eat, had a shower and got ready to go to see John. Before she left, she went to check the post-box to see if there were any letters. She found two. One was a get well card for John and the other one had an Irish stamp on it. It was addressed to her and John. It was from a firm of solicitors, M. B. Cantwell.

Kate remembered that this was the solicitors John's family used back in Ireland. It suddenly came into her head that Tommy had said at one stage that he would have a word with his solicitor to see about her and John making a claim against the British Army over the shooting. But with all that was going on with John, she had forgotten all about it. But obviously Tommy hadn't. The letter read:

"We have been informed by our trusted client Thomas Grugan that you would be interested in pursuing a personal damages claim against the British Army for the shooting of you both at the checkpoint on Carron's Road last January. From the knowledge we already have, we think there is a good case for compensation. We are just letting you know the situation. If you feel you wish to pursue the matter, we would have to speak to both of you in confidence. We will leave this matter with you. If you wish to contact us, you will find our details at the top of the page."

Kate hadn't given this much thought. *I'll discuss it with John when I go in*, she thought. She made her usual call to the shop on the way, and when she parked and went to the door of the clinic, sure enough there was John standing against the wall waiting for her. When they got to the cubicle, they had their usual cup of tea.

"Now, John, I have a bit of news for you tonight." She took the letter out of her bag and showed it to him.

John read the letter slowly. "Tommy never gives up on anything," he said. "What do you think about this whole thing?" he asked Kate.

"John, I don't know," Kate said. "The letter is as big a surprise to me as it is to you. It would be great to get compensation, especially for you as you are going to carry this burden for the rest of your life. Sure, there would be no harm in making contact with the solicitors anyway." John agreed, and Kate said she would do that in the next couple of days.

John went on to tell her that Nigel went home that morning, and he was actually missing him for the bit of crack. He thought by the way the physio was talking that he would be getting home himself in another few days. Kate returned home thinking about the whole business of compensation and contacting solicitors.

Chapter 31

By coincidence, the next day Jenna rang around half twelve. Lucky enough, Kate was in the office. She had rung to see how John was getting on. She said Tommy and Mary were wondering how he was, and she decided herself that the best way to find out was to give Kate a ring. Kate related how John was managing great with the prosthetic limb and how he thought he would be getting home in a couple of days. Jenna thought this was great and said she'd tell Tommy the good news when she saw him that night. Kate asked her if she knew that Tommy had contacted the solicitors on their behalf. Jenna said Tommy had said a little bit about it, but her personal opinion would be that they would be mad in the head not to put in a claim for injuries.

"Sure, if you don't succeed, you have nothing to lose."

When Jenna got off the phone, Kate was convinced that the right thing to do was to claim. At that, the phone rang again. It was just one o'clock. Kate answered and the voice said, "This is Clive. Same place, next Saturday. Be half an hour earlier as there is a stop on the way." At that, the phone went dead.

Kate thought, *If I hadn't enough in my head today with all the talk about the solicitors and now this*. She rang her Dad to see if he and Mum could go in and see John tonight. They were only too pleased to oblige.

She just felt she could do with an evening off after all this commotion.

When she got home from work that evening, and after eating, she poured herself a small drink and sat back to watch a film on the telly. With the worry of the day and the effects of the drink, Kate fell asleep and didn't wake until the film was long over. There was some chat show on which was dubbed with French subtitles. She turned the telly off and went to bed.

The following night when she went in to see John, he greeted her with a big smile. "You'll not have to come here anymore, Kate," he said. "I'm getting home tomorrow."

Kate threw her arms around him. "That's great, John. Oh, I can't wait to have you back in the house with me. Sometimes it can be very lonely, especially if I can't sleep."

"They tell me it could be tomorrow after dinner, but leave it until you finish work. Another couple of hours will make no difference," John

206

said. Kate thought this would be best as she had a busy day tomorrow and might find it hard to get time off.

John then explained that there would be people around to make adaptations to the house in the next couple of weeks to help with his incapacity. She went on to tell him that Jenna rang and what she had said about the compensation claim. He was anxious to know how everyone was at home and he was happy to hear they were all doing well.

Before Kate went home, she went up to the reception with John. She told the nurse John had been informed he was getting home tomorrow afternoon. She asked if it would be all right to collect him at half six. The nurse said that would be no bother as long as she was there before eight o'clock, as that was the time the night staff came on, and they didn't sign anyone out to go home. She went home in the best of form.

The next evening, when she was finished work, she went straight to collect John. One of the nurses had all his belongings packed waiting in the hallway. John was sitting on a chair beside them. The nurse told her to pull around to the side door as it would be less of a walk with all the stuff. When she took the car around, the nurse was standing with the door open. They both loaded everything into the boot. "I have just a couple of forms for John to sign and you can be on your way,"

With the forms signed, they were ready to go. John produced a bag. "Here you are, Heather," John said to the nurse. "There's a bag of biscuits and sweets I had left in my locker. I want you and the rest of the staff to have them. It's all I can offer you for all the attention you all gave me while I was here."

Heather threw her arm around him. "John, you were an exceptional patient, and we hadn't a minute's bother with you. Now you concentrate on getting yourself fully mobile again. And everyone here wishes you a full recovery." She put her arm around Kate. "Kate, look after John; you are a good couple."

Kate walked slowly to the car with John. When he got to the car, he looked around. "Glad to be out of there," he said.

When they got home, Kate led John into the sitting room. "Stay there, John, and I'll take your stuff out of the car." This took her a while. She then realised how much help the nurse had been when they were loading it. She just put everything in the hall, thinking she'd sort it out tomorrow evening. With this job done, she realised that she had no dinner this evening and was feeling peckish. Having already decided in her head that she wasn't cooking, she made her mind up to get a takeaway. She went into John and told him what she was intending to do and asked him if he wanted anything.

"Well now, Kate," John said, "I have survived on hospital food this last while and I just think I'll have a curry and chips. And what's more, I'll go with you for the spin."

Kate smiled and thought to herself, there's a man glad to be home. Away they went. Kate went in to get the food and John remained in the car.

When they finished eating, John insisted he'd do the bit of washing-up. He told Kate to go in and watch the telly and have a rest. Kate thought to herself that John might be still a little slow walking, but his mind was well alert. When John eventually came into the sitting room, Kate told him they would have a little homecoming drink and she went out and poured two drinks. They then sat on the couch and talked about what had happened and about their life in general. They talked until it was time for bed. This was the first time that Kate had seen John take off his limb before getting into bed. She found it intriguing. When he eventually got into the bed, she jumped in, too. She cuddled up to him and a tear came to her eye. *At last, I have him home.*

Chapter 32

The next morning, she rose for work, had a shower and was about to give John his tea in bed when he appeared in the kitchen beside her. "John," Kate said, "you gave me a fright. I was going to bring your tea down to you."

John told her that he had been in bed that long this past while that he just wanted to get up and get moving. He told her if the weather stayed good, he would walk around the garden today to practise his walking.

She kissed him and headed off to work. That evening after tea, John asked her if she would help him to have a bath because it was very difficult to get into the bath when he took off the prosthetic limb. She went and ran the bath and left two fresh towels out for him.

When the bath was ready, she helped him sit on the side of the bath and lower himself in. It was quite difficult. She left the door open and told him to let her know when he was finished. When he was done, he called her, and she helped him back out of the bath and gave him a hand to dry himself. She left him to fit his limb back on, as he was very capable of doing it on his own. When he came back up to the sitting room, they just sat and watched telly until bedtime.

Kate was glad to see Friday evening. On the way home, she went into the chip shop and got two fish and chips for herself and John. When she got home, she was surprised to see that John had the table set for the meal. "John," she said, "there's no call for you to do this."

"Look, Kate," John said, "I was told to exercise as much as I could, and there's nothing stopping me carrying a bit of cutlery and a few knives and a few plates with me. Anyhow, you are out working all week; any bit of help I can give you makes you job easier."

Kate smiled, thinking to herself, *It's a waste of time talking to him as he is determined to get back walking normally.*

When dinner was over, she went and had a shower. She was just drying her hair when it hit her. She had put it in the back of her head all week since the phone call. Jesus, she thought, it's tomorrow. When she eventually got back up to the sitting room, John was having a drink. He had one sitting waiting for her as well. "Here, Kate, come and join me," John said. "We might have a good few tonight."

"I don't know," Kate answered, letting on she had a pain in her head. She had to make the excuse as she didn't want a fuzzy head in the morning. "I'll try this and see how I feel," she said to soften the blow.

She drank her drink slowly and when she was finished she said she would go to bed as she wanted to be right for work in the morning. John said he'd wait up a while as he wasn't ready for sleep.

She heard John coming to bed as she wasn't asleep. She slept very little during the night, and when morning came, she got up and got dressed. She thought John was asleep when she got up, but she wasn't very long in the kitchen before he appeared. John asked how she was feeling this morning. She lied and told him she had a good night's sleep, and she felt a bit better this morning. She had hoped he wouldn't have gotten up this morning in case he copped how nervous she was. She kissed him and headed off for work.

She could feel herself all uptight as she headed into the office. There were a few extra problems to get solved before she hit the road. All of a sudden it was time.

As she got into the van, she wondered if she was right in the head. She thought of Clive, who she sort of liked. She thought what the consequences might be if she let him down. As she came into town, she wondered if it would be Clive. Would they send someone else, someone she mightn't know or get on with? As she approached the phone box, she breathed a sigh of relief. There was Clive standing inside the phone box. She found a parking space just past the phone box. She thought that she might be in a risky business, but at least he was someone she could trust, or at least she thought she could.

Clive got into the van after a few minutes. "When you come to Trentwood Roundabout, take a left turn, then travel on for about five miles and I will give you further instructions." That's all he said for now.

When she came to the roundabout, she did as he said. When they had travelled the five or so miles, he pointed to a large tree on the right-hand side of the road. "When you reach that tree, turn left down the lane and continue to the end of it."

It was a very long lane. If you didn't want anyone to see you doing something wrong, this definitely was the place to be, Kate thought. They must have travelled a mile down this lane. At the bottom there was a big old shed.

As they approached the shed, two old galvanised doors were pulled open. Kate couldn't see anybody and she thought whoever was pulling those doors were hiding behind them as they didn't want her to see them. "Drive up to the back wall," Clive said. "Switch the van off and stare straight at the wall. Do not look around you." At that, he got out of the van.

Kate stared hard at the front wall, afraid to even move an eyeball. She could feel herself sweating profusely. There was a bit of a silence. Then she heard the rear doors of the van being opened and someone got in. She heard something being placed on one of the shelves. She heard someone leaving the van and the doors were banged shut.

In a very short time, Clive got back in beside her. "Reverse back out and head back up the lane and we will head for our destination," he told her. She did exactly as she was told, and very soon they were at their destination.

Kate opened the gate and drove in. She got out to collect her containers and Clive got into the back of the van and returned with a container exactly the same as the ones she was collecting. "We'll not be taking this one home with us," Clive said with a wry smile. He disappeared up through the building and was missing for a good ten minutes. When he returned, he helped Kate load up the rest of the containers and they were done. Kate locked up and headed for home.

When they reached the town, she pulled up at the phone box to let Clive out, and he turned to face her. "It was nice working with you, but I have to tell you once again, any loose talk to anyone would have dire consequences. Good luck in your life." He jumped out and banged the door, walking straight across the street without looking back. As she watched him go, she thought to herself that she would probably never see him again.

Kate continued to the rest of the barracks to collect their containers. She dropped her containers off in the store and headed for home. She was so nervous with Clive and his absent friends that she felt she needed a good shower when she got home. John came to the door to greet her when she pulled into the yard. He kissed her when she got to where he was standing. When they went inside, she told him she was going to have a shower.

Whilst in the shower, she thought she could get the smell of someone cooking. When she came out of the shower, she could see that John was busy in the kitchen. When he saw her, he smiled. She noticed the table was set. "Sit down, Madam," John said, pointing to the chair at the top of the table. "I have your favourite meal." Going to the oven, he took out two plates and placed one in front of her and put his own down at his own place.

"Steak and chips," Kate said. "John, you are so good, but you are really doing too much. You are so good."

"Kate, I have told you I am not going to lie down with this limb. I intend to get back as near possible to normal as I can. And something else I am going to tell you, Kate. I think when we finish up here, we'll ring a taxi and go down to the Black Lion for a couple of drinks. I haven't had a pint in the pub in a long time."

Kate smiled and said, "What a way to finish off the day." Thinking what a way to finish off the day she was having.

They rang for the taxi and when it arrived, they headed off.

Chapter 33

Kate woke the next morning the worse for wear after her night out. John had turned on the radio as he liked to hear the news; a habit he had got into when he was in hospital. Kate decided she would get up and make her and John two cups of tea. She had just plugged in the kettle and gone to open the kitchen blind when she heard John shouting for her.

She rushed to the room, thinking what could be wrong with him?

When she opened the bedroom door, John burst out, "Kate, Winston Churchill Territorial Barracks in Barrow was blown up last night."

Kate didn't know whether she was going to wet herself or vomit.

"There were no casualties, but a lot of damage to neighbouring buildings," John continued.

She didn't realise it would happen so quick. "My God," she said, "I was there today. I could have been killed." She had to lie to compose herself and act natural to John.

"The IRA have claimed responsibility," John said. "Tommy will be in his glory back home."

Not as much as Clive will, she thought to herself. Kate said she'd go back up and make the tea.

She re-boiled the kettle and, getting out the cups, she reminded herself of all the times she h a d thought about nothing else, only that barracks, and now it had happened she didn't know how to think. When she took the tea down to the room, John was already getting up. She saw him strapping on his prosthetic limb and she thought to herself she was right to do what she had done. She took the tea back up to the kitchen. John joined her as she opened the blind to look at the early sunshine beaming in the window. *What a nice day*, Kate thought.

Kate thought that it would be good for her and John to have a spin down to the lakes and maybe get something to eat at the lakeside café. They were driving along in the sun and listening to the music on the car radio when there was a break in the music. The voice announced, "This is a newsflash. A bomb has exploded in an Army surplus store in Queen Street in London. A number of civilians have been injured. The building has been completely destroyed and will have to be demolished. The IRA have claimed responsibility."

"Jesus," John said, "the IRA have some people working well for them in this country." Kate could feel herself blushing. She was glad John was looking straight ahead. "There'll be bonfires over at home," John said.

"Yes, John, but the soldiers will be in a very nasty mood, which won't bide well for the Irish people," Kate said, trying to stem John's sudden interest in the IRA. She felt if she could change the subject she could relax and put to the back of her head the happenings of the last two days.

She drove on until she spotted the first restaurant on the journey. "Let's have lunch here, John," Kate said. "I'm feeling peckish." John loved this area and was quick to agree.

They went in and ordered their meal. In this particular café there was a great display of goldfish in large tanks and people spent their time admiring these fish while waiting on their meal. John and Kate really enjoyed looking at the different fish. They finished their meal and carried on their way around another few lakes, returning home around eight o'clock.

They listened to the nine o'clock news and Kate nearly fell out of her chair. "A man has been arrested in connection with the Winston Churchill Barracks bomb. He is being held by police for questioning at the minute."

Kate didn't hear the rest of the news, she was that much in shock. She couldn't let John see how she felt, and when the news finished, she told him she was tired and was going to bed. He said he'd sit another while. Kate went down to bed, but there was no fear of her sleeping. Who was this man who had been arrested? Was it Clive? No, it couldn't be. He would be smarter than that. Would it have any connection to her? No, Clive wouldn't talk. She remembered the stern warning he had given to her. Sleep wasn't plentiful that night.

Chapter 34

Monday morning, she got ready for work, giving John his breakfast in bed before she left. On her drive to work, she had made up her mind to tell anyone who asked that she just did her usual call on Saturday and there was nothing unusual that she had seen. Clive's warning was printed on her forehead.

When she went to her office, she carried out her usual Monday morning bits and pieces. It wasn't long before the Managing Director came into the office. "Good morning, Kate," he said. "You have probably heard the bad news about Winston Churchill Barracks the other night."

Kate went into a silence and started to shake. "Timothy, I was in that barracks on Saturday morning," she said, and she dropped into the chair, letting on to be badly shaken. "I could have been killed."

Timothy put his arm around her. "Come on, Kate," he said, "pull yourself together. Come on down to my office and we'll get you a cup of tea."

While they drank the tea, the Managing Director asked her if she had seen anyone or anything strange while she was there. Kate said she was in a hurry to get her work done and never noticed anything out of the way. He told her the police were asking if anyone that was there had seen anything. He told her that he had sent a technician in to fix a catering machine and when he told the police this they went and arrested him that evening, but they had to release him during the night as he didn't have a clue about what they were talking about. He said he thought they had a cheek to arrest him, so he wasn't even going to mention Kate was there as she had seen nothing anyway and she had enough to manage with John being less abled. Kate kept her act up, but a great weight had been lifted off her shoulders. But she got a nice surprise when the Managing Director told her to take the day off as he would get someone to fill in for her.

She went home in a lot better form than she went to work. She told John she wasn't feeling well, and she was going to go to bed for a while. She climbed into the bed determined to recoup the sleep she lost last night.

Kate went back to work feeling a lot happier that she was off the hook, but the only drawback about the bombing was that all the barracks were now tightly monitored with greater security. This meant she would be delayed a good bit at each barracks as all vehicles and personnel were being thoroughly checked on entry. This meant that Kate was ending up working longer hours, especially on a Saturday.

All across Britain, security had tightened up all over and all the major media were reporting how the British people were fed up with disruption to their lives both with the explosions and extra security on a lot of buildings. There were a lot of whispers of new talks between the British and the Republican Movement. But at this stage they were only whispers.

Kate's thoughts were diverted a bit with the news they had received in another letter from M. B. Cantwell solicitors when they had asked them to go ahead and make a claim against the British Army for their injuries. The solicitors requested that Kate and John have a personal meeting with them as soon as possible. John and Kate decided they would travel over the following weekend. They could catch the last flight on the Friday evening and come back on Sunday evening, meaning that Kate would only have to miss Saturday off work.

The solicitors didn't work on a Saturday, but because of the circumstances they said they would meet them on Saturday morning for whatever time it would take to sort things out.

John was really excited at the thought of seeing them all at home.

Chapter 35

That Friday night, Kate got home from work and John had grub ready for her. She had packed their luggage the night before, so all she had to do was have a shower and change her clothes. She carried the case out to the car. John would love to have done this, but she was afraid he might fall. John locked up and they were off to catch the plane.

When they landed in Ireland, they quickly got through security as there weren't many on the flight. When they got to the front entrance, Jenna and John's mother Mary were waiting on them. They all hugged each other, and they headed for Jenna's car. When they got home, Tommy was in the sitting room. He jumped up and firstly threw his arms around John and then went over to Kate. "Jaysus, yous are safer over here than in England, with all of them bombs going off," Tommy said, laughing. "Kate, you didn't want to be here when you came first, and it's more dangerous now to be in your own country." Tommy gave her a big wink and she knew he wasn't slagging her but letting her know that he was happy with the job she was tasked with. Mary, as usual, made the tea.

After the tea, Tommy thought they should go for a drink, but both John and Kate declined as they felt they wanted to be ready and alert for their meeting with the solicitors tomorrow morning. They all agreed they'd leave it until tomorrow night.

After a while, Kate said she'd get the case in from the car. Jenna told her the car wasn't locked. As she went out, Tommy said he'd help her. She knew he wanted to talk to her. They were only out the door when he said to her, "What a fucking job you done. The boys thought you were like a professional. The Brits are under pressure to start negotiating again because of people like you. Thanks, Kate."

At that, Jenna came out. "I better lock that car this time in case them Brits are lurking about. I heard you and Tommy talking. Did he tell you the good news?"

Kate looked puzzled. "What good news?" Kate asked.

Jenna took Tommy by the hand. "Kate, we are expecting our first baby."

"What?" said Kate. "This is great news!" She threw her arms around both of them. "I am going to tell John."

"Now, I am only a couple of months gone and haven't told Tommy's mother yet. We were waiting to tell you all tonight, but as one woman to another, when I saw you here, I couldn't keep it in any longer. Come on," Jenna said. "We may as well go in and tell Mary and John now."

When they went in, John and Mary were deep in conversation. Jenna spoke. "Mary and John, Tommy has an announcement to make." Tommy looked at her. "Go on, Tommy. They are waiting on the good news."

Tommy stuttered for a bit. "Jenna and I are expecting a baby."

The tears welled up in Mary's eyes and she went over and threw her arms around Jenna. John got up and threw his arms around Tommy. "Jesus, I'm delighted for you, our lad," John said.

Mary dried her eyes. "Well, no matter what anyone thinks about tomorrow morning, this evening has been a bloody great evening for me. First, I see my son back walking again, which I personally never thought I would; and then I'm told that I'm going to be a granny. This can't go without a little celebration. One or two will do yous no harm.

No one dared refuse Mary when she was in this mood. She went to the cupboard and produced the bottle. "Jenna, maybe you'll bring over the glasses," Mary said. "I suppose a drop of mineral will do you in your condition." Jenna smiled and went for the glasses.

They had a couple of drinks, but Kate and John said they'd stop at two. After a while, Tommy and Jenna headed for home and John and Kate decided to call it a day. When they got to the room, John said to Kate that she hadn't seemed too surprised when Tommy said about their new baby. He asked if it was because she couldn't get pregnant herself. She smiled and told him Jenna had already told her outside. She kissed him and told him, "We'll have our day, too, John."

The next day, John and Kate were in really good time for their appointment with the solicitors. Jenna drove them in. When they arrived, there was no sign of anyone and the door to the office was locked when they tried it, but shortly after a white Mercedes pulled into the car park. A tall man with a beard got out and went inside. Kate and John went over to the door and rang the bell. Straight away the same man with the beard opened the door. "Kate and John?" he asked.

"Yes," John said.

"Come on in. Glad to see you both." He explained that they didn't leave the door open on Saturday as they only dealt with whatever cases were booked in, and theirs was the only one booked in today. "My name is Shane Gardner," he said. "My speciality is compensation claims, and unfortunately lately most of them are against the British Army. Saying that, most of them are assaults by the Brits on civilians, wrongful arrests, etc. We haven't had anything as serious as your case, especially John, who has suffered this terrible injury.

"Now," he said, opening up a file, "we have whatever information you have furnished us with already in your correspondence. But we have a lot more to gather up. The first and most important thing is to give us the name of the man who came on the scene."

John told the solicitor the man's name was John Carter and they were not sure of his exact address, but they would get it and send it on to him.

The solicitor went on to tell them that they would need to gather a lot of information, such as all the treatment they had, length of time spent in hospital, length of time John spent in the prosthetic clinic, loss of earnings for both of them and a load of other things, so it might take a bit of time to put a substantial case together. "Not taking away from your case, Kate, but John's claim is an awful more complicated considering the severe disability he has suffered and how it will affect him for the rest of his life.

"At one time, compensation claims against the British Army were almost a waste of time, but lately we have been having some success, and especially in severe injury claims. So, we'll keep our heads up and take them on, hoping we will win both your cases and get the compensation you are definitely entitled to. I will be in constant contact with you over the next while and we will leave no stone unturned." He stood up and shook both their hands and accompanied them to the front door.

On their way home, Jenna asked how they had got on. John and Kate said they were very happy with how the solicitor had met them and he seemed to be on top of his game. Kate was saying not to count their chickens before they hatched, but she was confident that if anyone could win their case, Shane Gardner could.

They pulled into the yard at John's mother's house. Jenna parked in her usual spot. Kate looked at the car parked up in the corner of the yard. "Jesus, John, Meabh's here," she said.

John stared in that direction. "Come on," he said. He seemed so excited. Even with his prosthetic limb, he got there ahead of Kate. "Well, holy Jesus," John said, throwing his arm around

Meabh. He then embraced Paul. "Long time no see you, ye boy you."

Kate went over and shook hands with Paul. "Good to see you, Paul; you are looking well."

Meabh said that when she found out they were coming home this weekend, she persuaded Paul to get a man in to look after the farm for a couple of days. "And what did you do with wee Seamus?" Kate asked.

"Kate, just like at Christmas, Ma has taken charge of him and at the moment she's down in the room giving him a bottle and putting him off to sleep. You'll see him later on. You'll see some change in him."

"Ah, and now Tommy and Jenna are going to have their new baby," Kate said. "God, John, we'll have to try a bit harder!" she continued.

"Your time will come, Kate," Paul said.

The crack was great all day and when little Seamus appeared after his sleep, the three women nearly fought with each other over who would nurse him.

That evening, Tommy and Jenna arrived and announced that they were getting Chinese for the whole family to celebrate the announcement of their new arrival. Jenna had a pen and paper and took down the order. Paul and Tommy were going to get it.

On the way out, Tommy said to John, "You better come, too, in case we get lost."

The three of them headed off to the takeaway and John found out why Tommy told him to come, too. Tommy went in to order and when he came back he told the two boys that the man behind the counter said they were very busy, and it could be at least half an hour before the order would be ready. "Why waste a good half hour?" he said. "It will go quicker in the pub." The quick pints went down a treat.

After they had their meal, everyone gave a hand cleaning up and Kate grabbed her chance to get holding wee Seamus. The men were at a loose end and Mary read the situation. "Why don't you all go down to the pub for a drink and not have these fellows shuffling about? There's nothing worse than a man shuffling about in need of a drink. I'll mind the child."

Jenna said she'd ring 'Taxi' to come in about an hour's time. That give the girls time to get ready.

With the girls out of the room, Tommy and Paul started talking about the present situation with the Brits. John hadn't much interest, but he was surprised to hear that the checkpoints were well cut back. Tommy said there was a lot of talk of strong negotiations between the Brits and the Republican Movement. No one really knew much, but things had got a lot quieter. He added that it seemed since the bombs went off in England the British people were pushing for renegotiating of the ceasefire. "Of course," he said, "there are Republicans who don't want a ceasefire, and that's another problem."

The girls had by now all returned to the kitchen, and that stunted Tommy's talk. John thought to himself that with less security, Tommy would find it easier to get about.

With everybody ready to go, it was just a matter of waiting on the taxi. Just at that, 'Taxi' tooted the horn outside. They all left, and Mary settled in to mind her greatest asset, little Seamus.

When John was getting out of the taxi at the pub, 'Taxi' commented on how well he was able to walk with his new limb. "Hard to keep a good man down, 'Taxi'," he said.

They sat up at the top of the lounge. There were two fellas playing on the stage at the other end of the lounge. They were very good. As the night wore on, a lot of people came over to talk to John, especially commenting on how well he was and how they were glad to see him. Jenna wasn't drinking, and she must have been bored. "Come on, you two," she said, pulling Meabh and Kate out of their seats. "If I can't bloody drink, I can surely dance." She headed for the small dance area near the stage. The two others followed after her. Tommy shouted to her to mind herself. "Ah, dry your eyes, Tommy," she shouted back, laughing.

The night went on and the drink was flowing, and when the bar closed Jenna rang 'Taxi'. He said he would be half an hour as he was very busy. Eventually, 'Taxi' came back and they all headed home. Tommy seemed very relaxed all night and had a lot to drink, but when he went to get out of the taxi, he slipped and fell out on to the ground. He was holding his leg, saying it could be broken. Out of character, John started laughing, saying to Tommy, "God, don't worry, Tommy, if that leg's fucked, you can borrow mine when I'm not using it."

Meabh and Kate burst out laughing. Jenna, with the help of 'Taxi', got Tommy back on his feet. As the taxi pulled off, Jenna got them all together. "Now, you might be all pretty drunk, but not a word when we go in here or we will waken the child." Jenna waited until everyone had headed to bed. Then she linked Tommy, who was limping badly, out to the car to head home.

The next morning, everybody was slow to rise. Mary had taken the child up from Meabh's room as he had whimpered, looking to be fed. Kate came up to the kitchen a while after that. She was glad their flight wasn't until evening time as it would give her time to get her senses together. John appeared shortly after, and Kate put on the kettle. She just had the tea made when Paul and Meabh appeared. "Jesus, a drop of that tea would go down well," Paul said. Kate poured tea for everyone.

"I wonder how poor Tommy is?" Meabh said.

"What happened to him?" Mary asked.

"Ah, Ma, he slipped getting out of the taxi."

"We know why that was," Mary answered.

"Ah, he'll be all right," Meabh said, taking the child off Mary. "I'll take this fellow, Ma, and change his nappy, and he'll probably go for a sleep."

Mary started to prepare the dinner and Kate gave her a hand. Paul and John went out for a walk around the yard, more to settle their heads than anything else. John went over to the gate and looked up the road, and there they were, a foot patrol. He went back into the yard. As they passed the gate, one of the soldiers saw them. "All right, lads?" he said to Paul and John. They never let on they were there. "You two cunts deaf?" he said.

At that, the two lads headed back into the house. John could hear Paul muttering, "Shower of British bastards."

"What's up?" Meabh inquired.

"Aw, them cunts are going down the road," Paul told her.

Mary went out to the front to check where they went. "They are away across Kelly's field, heading for the far road. I'll ring Tommy and let him know."

The day went fairly quickly, and Tommy and Jenna appeared to take John and Kate to the airport. Tommy's ankle was heavily strapped as he had been to the hospital, and they told him that he had badly sprained it. The two were leaving at five o'clock to be in time for the flight. Kate was talking to Jenna and said she didn't know if she and John would be back before the baby was born, but she wished her all the best.

They all went to the yard when John and Kate were getting into Jenna's car. Meabh was holding little Seamus and Kate went over and gave him a big hug before she got into the car. They were on their way, and everyone waved them off.

Chapter 36

Kate had set off for work on Monday and at about eleven o'clock the phone rang. John answered it to hear a lady's voice asking him if he was John Grugan. He told her he was, and she proceeded to inform him that she was ringing on behalf of the British Disabilities Service and that his name was down to have facilities fitted in his house to help him with his disability. She said there was a slot this Wednesday for the engineer to come and inspect the house to see what needed to be done, and she asked him if that would be suitable. John told her there was no problem as he would be at home all day. She told him it would be in the morning, and it wouldn't take very long. He thanked her and got off the phone.

Kate was happy for John as she thought while he was doing very well getting around, some of these facilities might make life a bit easier for him.

The engineer came on Wednesday and looked at the whole house inside and out and noted everything he thought John would need.

When he was finished, he showed John the list and John said he was happy enough. He said it was usually about a month before the men would be there to fit everything.

To John's surprise, he told him he should also apply for a disability car as he would be entitled to it. He said it was a different department to his, but he gave him a phone number and told him to ring straight away and fully explain his case. He wished John all the best and left.

When Kate came home, John had dinner ready for her and proceeded to tell her all about the engineer coming and all the appliances he was going to get, and then he told her about the engineer giving him the number to apply for a disability car. Kate thought this was a brilliant idea as she knew John was missing his bit of independence in not being able to drive. "Why don't you ring them tomorrow, John, and put the wheels in motion?" John said he'd ring first thing in the morning.

There was very little talk from the media about the Troubles in Northern Ireland, and things had gone so quiet people were starting to question if there was something big going on behind the scenes. Then it dominated the news all over the world.

"After long and protracted re-negotiations, the Irish Republican Movement has entered a new deal with the British Government for all its units to cease hostilities as and from midnight tonight. Anyone breaking this agreement will be held responsible.

Signed: P. O'Neill."

John and Kate were watching a documentary on the life of Elvis Presley when the programme was interrupted by a newsflash. The same statement was read out. Kate was taken aback when she heard it.

"My God," John said, "Tommy and the boys will be happy with that, Kate. Isn't it great news for them?"

Kate agreed. But it put her back thinking about the barracks being blown up and Clive. She thought how much attention John was now giving to the political situation, whereas he never even commented on any of it before he was shot. Her thoughts rambled on in her head so much that she didn't realise until the credits came up that the film had ended.

Back home, Tommy wasn't surprised at the statement being released, as those that needed to know were kept well informed. He wouldn't have known the exact time, but he knew it was imminent. The Brits had pulled well back on their patrolling and things had gone very quiet on both sides.

Things didn't stay quiet for long. Jack Lavery rang Tommy the next evening. "I'll be at the old mill tomorrow evening at seven. I'd like to see you there." Tommy said he'd be there and hung up.

The next evening, Tommy arrived at the old mill and Jack was already there. Tommy went over and got in beside him in his car.

"What the fuck's going on, Tommy? The last time we called a ceasefire with these cunts, your own brother was nearly killed, and he has to spend the rest of his life on an artificial leg. Your sister-in-law could just as easily have been killed, too, and now here we are bowing to them again. Why are we doing this again?"

Tommy took a deep breath and tried to explain how everyone was aware that everything was leading to a permanent ceasefire. He told Jack he himself didn't know when it was coming, but knew it was going to happen.

The talks with the Brits seemed to have gone well, whereas the Republican Movement hadn't yet got all they were looking for. They were negotiating well, and to show trust they decided to cease hostilities.

"Tommy," Jack said, "that is stupid. We have got nothing yet and we shouldn't have declared a ceasefire until we have everything we wanted. If ever. Tommy, you know there's a lot of men in this area not happy with what's going on. Men who won't conform to this ceasefire."

"Jack," Tommy said, "as a member of the Republican Movement, I intend to abide by what I am told to do, and I think any volunteer worth his salt should do the same. As the man in charge, I intend to make sure everyone knows where he stands as far as this area is concerned. Go back and tell your buddies there is a meeting in Matties' loft on Friday night at eight. And tell them the usual precautions as ever."

Tommy got out straight away and left Jack to think about that one.

Chapter 37

The following Friday night, Tommy went to Matties' loft. There were more people there than he expected. But he was determined to put his point across. Once again, Jack Lavery took the lead, putting points across that Tommy was fed up listening to at this stage.

Other men came out with more strong points. A lot of the men came out in favour of the ceasefire, and then John Parsons put his hand up. John had done eight years in jail after being shot in a gun battle with the Brits just beyond Cregan's hill. "Listen, boys, Tommy has come here tonight to tell us what is happening as far as the Republican Movement is concerned. He has been told by them what to tell us. And as a true volunteer, he will carry out what he is told to. Let me tell all you boys here, Tommy Grugan was no slouch when it came to taking on the Brits, and believe me, if he says something he means it. We all know that we gave the Brits a good run for it, but we are never going to beat them.

"Do we want more men to go to jail, or not be able to stay at home two nights in a row or lie alone in an early grave like a lot of our friends are? Boys, listen to the Republican Movement. Listen to Tommy Grugan tonight."

"Jaysus, John," said Tommy, "you shouldn't make me out to be such a hero; you were a great volunteer yourself. All you men were great men in your own right; but, boys, the word has come back from the top. The word is that the negotiations are going very well. The bombs going off in England seem to have really annoyed the English people, and there is an awful pressure on the British authorities to get an agreement with the Republican Movement. The British have conceded on a number of our demands, and in return we have agreed to a cessation of all military operations for now. All weapons will be stored, and all dumps secured. We will monitor the situation, and if we are not successful in our negotiations, we will not be afraid to take up arms again. No breach of the ceasefire will be tolerated. Negotiations will continue until we get our ultimate goal, a United Ireland. Now, boys, remember. Be careful leaving here."

Before he had finished talking, he noticed Jack Lavery and about half a dozen others had rushed out the door. To allow men to leave at different times, a lot of men stood around waiting for their chance to go.

All around the place the talk was about the ceasefire. In the pubs, outside the chapel on a Sunday after Fr Hagan had given a long sermon on the great news of what he called the ceasing of a few individuals shooting at the Army. A lot of people gave him no heed as they thought to themselves, he never gave a sermon about any poor civilian who was killed or injured by the Army.

Back in England, John had just come back from the local shop when the phone rang. When he answered it, the lady informed him that the men could come and fit the disability equipment the following Monday if it was suitable. John said that it would suit fine. He told Kate when she came home that evening, and she thought this would be great for John as she had seen him push himself so hard that he could almost go walking anywhere now.

Sure to their word, the following Monday three lads came and got stuck into getting the work done. They worked very hard, and John kept them supplied with cups of tea, and he really enjoyed the crack.

The man in charge informed him that they would get the work completed in the one day, and before he left he took John around all the different pieces of equipment and showed him how to get the best use out of them. When they left, John thought that it was a great day's crack, and the day just flew. Kate came home and couldn't get over all the work that had been done, and with very little mess.

A couple of weeks later, John got confirmation of receiving his disability car. He was informed he would go and do a test to see if he was able to drive the car with his prosthetic leg, and if he wasn't they would have to fit hand controls for him, which they assured him would be no problem and there would be no extra charge. Once again, Kate was very happy with all the help John was receiving, as he was really pushing himself to get back to normal.

Kate took a half day as it was the day John was to go to get his test with his disability car. John seemed to be in great form, and when they went into the garage the manager showed him a lovely navy Nissan and his eyes lit up. The manager handed him the keys and told him in his own time to see if he was able to drive it around the yard with his prosthetic limb. Kate decided she'd stand and watch in case he felt nervous if she was in the car. After a short time when John seemed well able to drive, the manager beckoned him to pull over. "Listen," he said to Kate, "I have a bit of paperwork to get John to sign, so why don't you get in beside him there and take a wee spin around the town and I'll have everything ready when you come back?"

Kate looked at John and he was so eager to get out on the road. When he was on the road, he looked at Kate. "Kate, I know I'm driving a bit slow, but when I get this leg used to it, I'll give this yoke some gyp."

Kate laughed. "Just take it handy for now, John, as we want to get back in one piece."

After a tour of the town, they returned, and John signed all the necessary forms. Kate said she would follow him home in case he had any problems. The manager wished him all the best and told him if he had any problems with the car, just give him a ring.

When they got back home, Kate could see that John was thrilled with the car as he looked at every bit of it. He had the boot opened, showing her inside. He told her he thought the colour was lovely and he went on about it like a child with a new toy. It was then she realised what time it was. She had to be back at work in an hour. She told John she had to go.

Just when Kate and John thought nothing could have gone better this week with John getting his car, a couple of days later the phone rang. When John answered it, he was surprised to find it was his boss, Ray Timmins. Ray had been following John's recovery initially, but hadn't rung in a while.

"Well, John," Ray said, "how are you keeping? Long time no hear. How are you?"

John related how he was getting along well, and he told him about getting the new car. Ray wished him all the best with it. "Now, John," he said, "would you be at home on Friday night if I call round?" John said he would, but didn't know why Ray was calling and he didn't say.

When Kate arrived home, John told her about Ray phoning, and that he was calling round on Friday night. He told her he thought he might be coming to tell him that he wasn't fit to work anymore and he was letting him go.

Kate was puzzled, too. "John," she said, "if he is coming to tell you he thinks you're not fit for your job anymore because of your disability, just take it on the chin. With your will to get on, you'll find another job. Don't you let yourself get down over a bloody job."

It was about half seven on Friday night when the doorbell rang. Kate answered the door.

"Kate, it's great to see you."

"Come in, Ray, it's great to see you, too," she said.

"Ah, John, great to see you," Ray said, as he shook his hand. "You are looking well for all you came through. Here, there's a wee something to enjoy," he added, handing John a bottle of wine and a box of chocolates.

A peace offering before the dismissal was the thought that went through Kate's head. "Will you have a cup of tea or coffee, Ray?" she asked.

"I'd love a cup of coffee," he said.

They all sat down in the sitting room and Ray talked about all the happenings to John and Kate. He went on to tell John that all the people at work sent their best wishes. The talk dragged on for a good while and then he got round to it. "John," Ray said, "I have come for a reason." Kate knew it was coming. "Peter Finn, our office manager, has gone to another company, and that leaves us needing someone to replace him. How would you like the job?"

Kate looked at John. He was stunned. "Jesus," John said. "Ray, I thought you came to let me go."

Ray sat back. "John, why would I do that? You have been a great servant to our company. I was thinking about you, and I thought your disability might curb your ability to do your present job; and when this position came up, I realised it would be perfect for you."

"Will I be fit for it?" John said.

"Look, John," Ray said, "you will have a wee bit of re-training to do, but it will be no bother to you when you get the hang of it."

Kate spoke up. "Ray, if you'd seen the effort this boy put in to get back to where he is now, you can have no fear of him not being able to do this job. Ray, we are indebted to you for this."

Ray looked at John. "Now for the awkward question, John. When are you coming back to us?"

John looked at Kate. She shrugged her shoulders and smiled. "Up to you, John."

John scratched his head. "What about Monday week, Ray? If that's all right with you?"

"John, it's okay with me," Ray said.

They all shook hands and Ray was on his way. John put his arms around Kate and lifted the bottle of wine. "Will we celebrate with this?" he said, smiling.

Chapter 38

Back in Ireland, things had been generally quiet and on the whole people were happy that they could move about freely without the hassle of the British Army, and the quality of life was generally better. Tommy enjoyed being able to go to the football matches again, and some of his mates were trying to persuade him to tog out once again. But he had decided he had had too many birthdays at this stage to do that, thinking that he might get involved maybe on the committee. Another reason he didn't want to get involved in playing any more was that with Jenna pregnant he might get injured, and he didn't want that to happen.

All of a sudden, the peace and quiet was shattered.

It was a Friday evening and Tommy and Jenna were sitting in the stand, watching the lads playing Pawnstown in the first round of the championship. Pawnstown were the better team and had just gone in at half-time four points ahead. Jenna had just commented on how peaceful the evening was when a mighty bang ripped through the air. Everyone stood up to look around, but Tommy knew it was a good bit away.

"What the hell is that?" Jenna asked.

"It seems to be an explosion," Tommy said. "But we will have to wait to find out more."

People were gathering in groups, speculating on what had happened. Just at that, a helicopter flew across the pitch. The teams came back out for the second half, but Tommy's attention was no longer on the football. He was trying to figure out what the hell the explosion was about. He knew he couldn't leave early to find out what was up without drawing attention to himself. Jenna was shouting obscenities at some player who had fouled one of their players. Tommy's head was elsewhere. When the match was over, Tommy and Jenna headed home to Tommy's.

When Tommy got home, he rang Pat Dunne. He told him he'd meet him in the pub in half an hour. Tommy got there first, and as he was going to order a drink he noticed Pat coming through the door. He ordered two pints and both of them went over to a table at the far end of the bar where they could talk in peace.

Tommy asked Pat, "What's the story with this explosion, Pat? Did you hear anything?"

"No," Pat said, "I know no more than you; just that the bomb missed the cop car, but the driver lost control and went over the bank and the cops are badly injured. Tommy, I suspect it has something to do with Jack Lavery and his buddies, as when I was going into the shop a while ago, he was coming out. He grinned at me and asked me how the ceasefire was going. He was clearly gloating."

"He can gloat all he likes, but whoever carried out that operation missed their target, so there is nothing to gloat about there," Tommy added. "We'll have to see how the British react to this, as they won't know who carried this out. It could be all deals off with the Brits."

They had two more pints and then went their separate ways, saying if either heard any more they would have another discussion.

The mystery was solved very quickly. The next morning when the daily papers came out, the statement was on the front of every paper:

"The Real IRA detonated a landmine on the Pond Road last night. Unfortunately, the landmine missed its intended target. We will continue to target the British Army and all its cronies. They might not be as lucky the next time."

Tommy and the boys were glad that the peace negotiations went ahead, even though these sporadic attacks from the Real IRA kept happening. A type of trust had built up between both sets of negotiators, and some of the former activists were now striving to build a political base to succeed with upcoming elections. Tommy enjoyed this as he liked the camaraderie one built with people getting them on your side in order that they might vote Sinn Féin when the elections eventually came along.

Tommy's other big worry was that Jenna was almost about to have their baby. She was very tired lately and she was wishing the whole affair was over. Tommy was also kept very busy as he was renovating his Uncle Eamon's house. The house was on the far end of the farm, and as Eamon had never married, he left the house to Tommy when he passed away. There was a lot to be done to it, but the builders were going well, and Tommy hoped that it would be ready for him and Jenna to move into when Jenna had the baby.

He thought to himself he might be busy now, but he wasn't half as busy as he had been during the Troubles.

As time went on, the negotiations continued, and eventually the British granted an amnesty to all political prisoners. In order to set up a power-sharing assembly, a date for an election was agreed. People were selected as candidates for the various different parties. The local Sinn Féin

Cumann approached Tommy to stand as the local candidate, but Tommy was quick to tell them he thought they would be better selecting one of the younger men who had been released from prison. They would be better able to deal with all the hard graft an election would bring.

Most of these lads inside had studied political and educational courses and would be well able to debate any issues against their political opponents. Also, they would be more popular with the electorate. Some people would vote for them because they were sympathetic that they had been in jail, and others would vote for them because they considered them heroes.

The Cumann decided to nominate Raymond Curran as their candidate. He and his brother had spent eight years in jail. Raymond had almost qualified as a primary school teacher when the two boys were arrested shifting weapons over in the far country. It was felt with his popularity and good education that he would make a great candidate. It would take a massive amount of drive and determination to get him elected.

Chapter 39

Jenna had been staying with Tommy and Mary since she became pregnant, and Tommy didn't realise how handy this was to be until one night about eight o'clock when the two of them were watching a film and all of a sudden Jenna let out a shout. "Oh, Jesus, Oh my God." She started moving around on the couch. She stood up and grabbed her stomach and sat down again just as quickly. She winced in pain.

"What's wrong, Jenna, what's wrong?"

"I think the baby's coming," she said.

"Oh, holy Jesus," he said. "I'll get my mother." He ran up to the kitchen and told Mary, "I think the baby's on the way."

"What? Get out of my way!" she said, and rushed past him.

When she got to the kitchen, she could see that Jenna was in a distressed state. She got a cold damp cloth and placed it on her forehead. "Tommy, get the bag with Jenna's clothes in it and get the car over to the door."

"The bag, the car keys, the bag… I can't find the car keys!"

"Tommy, for God's sake pull yourself together; this girl has to get to hospital."

Tommy got the bag and the car keys.

"Right," Mary said, "I've rung the hospital. Let's get Jenna into the car."

Jenna got in the back and Mary got in beside her. Tommy hit the road in spots on the way to the hospital.

When they reached the hospital, Tommy pulled up at the Emergency door and Mary helped Jenna inside. Tommy went and parked the car and returned with Jenna's bag. She was taken straight away to the maternity ward. Tommy accompanied her and Mary waited outside in the waiting room.

About an hour had passed when Tommy came into the waiting room and threw his arms around his mother and gave her a big hug. "It's a girl, Ma, and do you know what? Jenna wants to call it after you." Mary sat back down and started to cry. Tommy put his arm around her. "Come on, Ma, I'll take you home."

On the way home in the car, Tommy said he was sorry that he wasn't more help to her when Jenna went into labour. "Look," Mary said, "yous are all big men until there's a bit of panic, and then yous just fall down. I don't know how yous got through the Troubles at all." He could see her smiling.

When they got home, Mary looked at Tommy. "We can't go to bed without wetting the child's head." Tommy smiled. Mother's excuse for a wee tipple. The two glasses were already on the table.

Tommy was up early the next morning and headed straight in to see Jenna and the baby. Jenna had just finished feeding little Mary when Tommy arrived, and the nurse was helping Jenna to change her. Tommy sat in the armchair beside the bed, proud as punch watching his two girls.

When they were finished, Jenna came over, gave him a big kiss and put the baby into his arms. He held her so tight in fear of dropping her.

"Relax, Tommy," Jenny said. "You'll not let her fall."

He examined her little arms and legs and looked at her chubby red face and thought how beautiful she was. Jesus, he thought to himself, how life had changed. He never thought he would have a beautiful moment like this.

A week had gone by, and when Tommy went in this night Jenna was all smiles. She told him she and the baby were going home tomorrow. Tommy had taken bars and sweets in from the shop and both of them sat there eating them. They talked away for a good while and then they were rudely interrupted by a cry from the child.

Jenna said she was looking to be fed and Tommy said he'd go on ahead and he would see her in the morning. He told his mother, and she was over the moon.

Tommy woke up the next morning to hear some sort of commotion. When he went up to the kitchen, his mother was rubbing the new cot they had got for the child, and she said, "Glad you decided to get up. I have to change that bed and when you get a minute, I want you to lift this cot down to the room. I'll be able to put it beside the bed when I have the bed changed. And here, look. I have that buggy nice and clean. You have to take that with you to the hospital in the morning."

Tommy put the cot down in the room. He had a bit of breakfast and decided to get ready to put Jenna and the baby's stuff in the car and stay offside until he collected them, as he had had enough of his mother's fussing for now.

He told Jenna he'd be in for her at twelve o'clock. And true to his word, he was there on time. He held the baby when Jenna went to get changed; and with all their belongings gathered up, they headed for home.

When they eventually got home, Mary was waiting for them and she went straight over and took the buggy off Jenna and took the child out, sat on the couch and nursed her. "If only your father was here now to see his grandchild," she said. Jenna smiled and thought to herself, *I won't have much work with this child.*

Chapter 40

Kate and John were thrilled to hear about the new baby. John thought it was great that they had decided to call it after his mother. They went out and bought a load of baby clothes and posted them off. John had started his new job and loved it. He had found it hard to get to grips with it at the start, but was really liking it now. The solicitor had been on to them, and he told them that, after a long time, he was finally making progress with their claim. He said that due to a slight change in the law, the British Army could no longer hide behind the smokescreen of confidentiality. He stated that where there were witnesses to an occurrence, the occurrence could be contested if the witnesses were prepared to swear under oath.

In times of conflict, some witnesses were afraid to testify in case of retaliation from the Army at a later stage. But, thankfully, he added that their witnesses were prepared to testify. So, he said he would be in touch as he would have to meet them again in Ireland. Kate and John put the whole thing to the back of their minds, thinking that it could be a long time, if ever, before there would be a final development. But with a good few correspondences back and forth, things started to take a life of their own.

Then, one Monday, John came home from work. He was waiting on a date from the local hospital to have his usual check on his leg. He went to the postbox to see was there. He picked up the envelope, but it looked very official. When he opened it, he couldn't believe his eyes. It was from his solicitors.

"For the attention of John and Kate Grugan. Your presence is required to attend Her Majesty's Crown Court in Grennanstown on the morning of 4th August. You are requested to be there at ten o'clock sharp. The case in question is John and Kate Grugan vs British Armed Forces."

John read it over and over again. He couldn't get his head around it. He left the letter on the table and started to prepare a bit of grub. It wasn't long before Kate arrived home. "Well, John," she said, "how did your day go?" John didn't get time to answer her when she said, "What's this letter about, John?"

"An invitation to the Hunt Ball in the Town Hall," he said jokingly, knowing that Kate detested blood sports.

"I'm going to no Hunt Ball, and neither are you!"

John smiled as Kate opened the envelope. She read it slowly. "John, Hunt Ball my eye!"

"Do you think this is going to work?" John asked her.

"Oh, John, I hope it works out for you," Kate said.

John was quick to answer. "You were shot, too; it's not all about me."

They cuddled each other and said it was the best news they'd had in a long time. Kate laughed. "If we win our case, we could be rich."

They booked a week off for that time well in advance. They were thinking it would be great to get home as they would be able to see Tommy and Jenna's baby; and, of course, be with Mary again.

The time dragged on, but eventually it arrived. They left two days earlier on the 2nd, just to make sure there would be no mishaps. They spent the day before the court case with Tommy and Jenna and the baby. Everyone was glad the trial was going ahead. Mary told them not to be too optimistic as the Brits always had a way of twisting the truth. Kate didn't feel as confident when she heard this, as she always thought Mary could see through most problems.

Shane Gardner had requested they meet him the evening before the case to instruct them what to say. When he met them in his office, he told them they had a great case, but he was putting them straight that there was no guarantee that they would win. He assured them he would do his very best, but the real positive they had and which the Brits weren't aware of was that they had two new witnesses who were working in the field beside where John and Kate were shot. They hid along the ditch on the day when they heard the shots. The Brits discovered them and gave them a good beating and told them that if they ever told anyone they would find them and shoot them.

One of these lads had to go to the hospital with a broken arm after the beating, and his hospital records would place him at the scene. Kate and John assured him they wouldn't tell a soul.

He then went on to explain to them that the British barristers would bully them when they were questioning them. "They'll put you under pressure to make a mistake. Take your time with your answers and always just tell the truth. You can't find a flaw in the truth," he told them. "You were there, they weren't. Be brave tomorrow. You both had to be brave to come through this, so repeat the dose tomorrow."

Shaking hands and with a big smile, he said, "See you both tomorrow."

The next morning, Kate was first up. When she showered, she came back to the bedroom to get dressed. John was lying staring at the wall. She realised she would have to help him shower as he hadn't got the aids for getting into the bath that he had at home. "I'll give you a hand in the shower, John, when I'm finished getting dressed." He thanked her, but she thought he was a bit subdued. "John, are you okay about today?" She didn't expect what came next.

John sat on the side of the bed and looked at her. "Kate, I could never fire a gun or probably never will, but I am getting the chance to beat the British Army tomorrow. I am not going to miss it. If some dirty British fucking barrister thinks he's going to break me to admit to his lies, he's in for an awful shock."

Kate just smiled. "Come on, I'll help you with the shower," she laughed.

The next morning, everyone in the house was up bright and early. Tommy was up helping Jenna with the baby. Mary was preparing breakfast when John and Kate came into the kitchen. They had their breakfast quickly and went to get ready for court. They wanted to look

their best to give a good impression to the judge.
Tommy and Jenna said they were going to court
to support them, as Mary had thought it a good
idea as she could mind the child. John and Kate
headed off as they wanted to be there early in case
Shane Gardner might want to talk to them.

On entering the courtroom, Kate thought it
was such an old, drab building. There were legal
teams on both sides of the room. There was a
group of people sitting together on a raised
platform at the top left-hand side of the room. She
would find out later that this was the jury who
would make the final decision on the court case.
Shane Gardner was over on the right-hand side
of the room with his team. When he saw them
enter the court, he approached them and
instructed them to sit in the centre of the court
near the front as they would be able to hear and
see everything from there. He told them it would
probably be another half an hour before the court
commenced. He told them when the judge
entered, they were to stand up, as this was the
custom and he didn't like it if people didn't. They
sat down and waited. Kate had never been in a
court before and she thought to herself that it was
far from what she had seen in films or on the
television.

Shortly afterwards, she noticed Tommy and
Jenna coming into the court. They sat over on the

left-hand side. When they spotted John and Kate, they waved over. Some other people came in and sat beside Tommy and Jenna. John waved over at them, and they waved back. He whispered to Kate that they were neighbours and they had probably come to support them.

Just at that, a man up at the long bench at the front of the court stood up and said in a loud voice, "All rise."

Everyone stood up, including John and Kate. At that, a tall man in a long white wig came up the middle aisle accompanied by a smaller man carrying a lot of reams of paper. They headed right up to the front and continued up the steps to sit at the bench. The man with the wig sat down at the middle of the bench and the other man sat on his left, spreading out his papers in front of him as he sat down. Kate thought the whole scene was like something out of a Dickens novel.

The judge took some papers from the bench and studied them. He looked into the body of the court over his glasses as if he was doing a head count that everyone was present. He then cleared his throat and started talking.

"Today we have a case in front of us where a very serious allegation is being made against members of our Armed Forces. . The first person I would like to call to the stand is the legal representative for the Armed Forces, Barrister Meredith."

A tall man rose from the body of the court. He was in full military dress. The smaller man at the bench handed him the bible and he swore to tell the truth and nothing but the truth. He tapped the microphone and started to talk. "Your Honour, I am here to defend two brave soldiers who are being recklessly accused of causing wilful injury to a Mr John Grugan and his wife Mrs Kate Grugan." He took a grip of his coat lapels and stuck out his chest as if he was an orator on the stage at the West End. "Your Honour, the truth of this story was very simple. On the twenty-ninth of January, a checkpoint had been set up on the Fern Road on information that there was going to be terrorist activity in that area on the morning in question. Mrs Grugan was stopped by the soldiers at the checkpoint. She showed her documents to the soldier when requested, but when the soldier proceeded around to the passenger side, John Grugan refused to show any identification. When the soldier asked him again, he grappled with the soldier and the soldier in question had to put him to the ground. After he was restrained, Mr Grugan reluctantly handed over his identification. After a reprimand, the soldier allowed them to drive off. As they drove off, shots were fired at the checkpoint. Unfortunately, the shots must have hit Mr and Mrs Grugan."

Kate would have loved to go down and box his jaw. He was lying through his teeth. She settled herself. The Barrister continued, "I would like to call Private John Stanhope as a witness."

A small, stout, red-haired, well-dressed man took to the stand. "Mr Stanhope," the Barrister continued, "you were in charge of this checkpoint on the day in question. Is that right?"

"I was, Your Honour," he answered.

"I want you to give a true account of what happened at that checkpoint that day."

The soldier gave the exact same account word for word as the Barrister. One would think they had learned it off by heart.

When he was finished, the judge told him to return to his seat. At that, Shane Gardner stood up. "Your Honour, I would like to call some witnesses for the defence."

"Go ahead," the judge said.

Looking over at John, Shane said, "I'd like to call Mr John Grugan."

John took the stand. The bible was produced again, and John swore on it. Shane started off. "John, I want you to relate to this court what exactly happened when you were stopped at this checkpoint on that day."

John told exactly what happened. How they asked him if he was Tommy Grugan and how they wouldn't believe him that he was John Grugan, and how they pulled him out of the car and manhandled him on the ground.

The soldier kicked him, and it was only when his wife intervened that they believed who he was. He went on to say how his wife had just driven away from the checkpoint when they were both shot.

At that, the Barrister stood up. "Mr Grugan, I find it extraordinary that a trained soldier in the British Army would pull you to the ground for no reason"

John stared at him and answered, "I said he didn't believe me that I wasn't Tommy Grugan."

"Had you no identification to show him?" the Barrister asked.

"I have already stated that I tried on several occasions to show him it and it was only with the intervention of my wife that he eventually looked at it."

"How do you know it was the soldiers who shot you?"

"The shots came directly after we drove away from the checkpoint."

"That doesn't mean that they were fired by the Army," the Barrister said, and sat down.

Shane was on his feet straight away. "Your Honour, I would like to call my second witness."

"Proceed," the judge said.

"I would like to call Kate Grugan."

Kate stood up, took the stand, the bible was produced, and Shane asked her to relate what happened at the checkpoint. She repeated all John had said. At the end, the Barrister stood up. "Mrs Grugan, you have also said shots were fired when you drove away from the checkpoint, but you can't prove who fired them."

Kate could feel her temper rising, but she knew she would have to hold her head. "I can't prove it for definite, but I know it was them."

"This country is full of illegal gunmen," the Barrister said. "It could easily have been some of them."

Shane rose to his feet quickly. "Your Honour, is this man telling us that any illegal organisation is going to chance being killed or injured by taking on a heavily supported Army checkpoint? Is this what he is saying?"

The Barrister jumped up. "Has the prosecution evidence to say that there were no illegal gunmen in the area? Have they? I doubt it."

Shane turned to the judge. "Your Honour, I would like to call my third witness."

The judge peered down at Shane. "Go ahead."

Shane called on John Carter. John took the stand and the oath. "Mr Carter, you were at this checkpoint on this same day, were you not?"

"I was," John answered.

"Mr Carter, could you explain to the court what you saw at that checkpoint on the day?"

"I had just pulled up to the checkpoint when I saw a car in front of me. A soldier was talking to a lady at the driver's window. He then went around to the passenger side of the car. He seemed very agitated and then I saw him pulling out a man by the neck and on to the ground. He seemed to have his knee on his chest. He then kicked him two or three times in the side. The lady who was driving ran around and was trying to stop the soldier kicking the man on the ground. She was showing something to him, something like a licence. She eventually got him back into the car and they were driving off slowly. I had my window down ready to show my licence when I was told to go on through. But as I went to move, a soldier on the ditch shouted 'Bastards' and fired some shots from his rifle."

The court was in complete silence. John Carter hesitated. He asked for a drink of water. The court clerk filled some from a jug on the table and handed it up to him. "What did you do at this stage, Mr Carter?" Shane asked.

John Carter composed himself. "I was startled, and I thought it was best to drive away from the danger."

The Barrister jumped up. "Mr Carter, you said you heard a trained soldier utter the word ' bastards'. You were in your vehicle. How could you hear this inside your vehicle?"

John looked annoyed. "I have already said I had my window open to hand my licence to the soldier. I distinctly heard what he said, and I distinctly heard the shots which nearly pierced my eardrums." John wasn't going to be intimidated.

Shane stood up. "Mr Carter, what happened when you drove away from the checkpoint?"

"I only got a couple of hundred yards when I came upon a car which had run in against a ditch. I stopped as I knew it was someone in trouble. When I got up to the car, I realised it was the same car that had been stopped at the checkpoint in front of me. When I got to the driver's door, the woman was trying to force it open to get out. I helped her out, and she was screaming, 'My husband, he's dead.' She pulled open the passenger door and the man was crouched in the footwell. I checked his pulse, and he was still alive. I told her I was going to drive them to the hospital. I went to help her into the back of the car when I could see she was bleeding badly from her arm. I drove as fast as I could to get to the local hospital and got them help. I feel if I hadn't done this the outcome would have been an awful lot worse."

The Barrister stood up. "You drove this car uninsured to the hospital. This in itself was breaking the law."

Shane jumped up. "This is utter madness what this man is trying to say. Of course anybody would go to any means to save someone's life. Your Honour, this line of questioning is futile."

"Stick to the case in question, Barrister," the judge said. "Have you any further questions for Mr Carter?"

The Barrister said he hadn't.

Shane was on his feet again. "Your Honour, I would like to call my fourth witness," he said.

"Granted," the judge answered.

"I would like to call Michael Toman to the stand."

A man stood up beside where Tommy and Jenna were sitting. Kate had never seen him before. He went up to the stand and took the bible and the oath.

"What is your occupation, Mr Toman?" Shane asked him.

"I am an agricultural contractor," Mr Toman answered.

"On this day in question, where were you working?"

"I was working on the Fern Road with an employee of mine, John Wilson. We were cutting hedges for a Mr Riley."

"Did you see a checkpoint on the road?"

"Yes, we were working and noticed nothing until the belt broke on one of the machines. This meant we had to stop to try and replace the belt. It was at this point we became aware of the soldiers at the checkpoint."

"Did you see any cars stopped at the checkpoint?" Shane asked.

Mr Toman continued, "We saw a car stopped at the checkpoint with a Murray's Hire sign on the side of it. There were two people in it.

"It was stopped for a few minutes and then a soldier came around to the passenger side. That soldier pulled the man out of the car and was kicking him on the ground. The woman came around and remonstrated with the soldier. The man and woman got back into the car and had just driven off when we heard another soldier screaming 'Bastards', and he opened fire at the car."

The Barrister jumped up. "Wait a minute," he said. "How do you know he was shooting at the car?"

"Well, he wasn't shooting ducks with yon big gun," Mr Toman answered. The people in the court burst out laughing.

"Order in the court," the judge said. "Any more of this behaviour and I will clear the court. Okay, continue with the questioning."

Shane asked Mr Toman, "What happened next, Mr Toman?"

He continued, "When we heard the shots and the soldier screaming, we ran in behind one of the machines for cover. One of the soldiers must have seen us, as the next thing we knew we were surrounded by soldiers. They knocked me to the ground. One soldier caught John Wilson and twisted his arm up his back so that they actually broke it. They made us lie face- down on the ground until the police came to investigate the incident. The police allowed us to go as they realised we were only working in the fields. I drove John Wilson straight to the hospital."

The Barrister stood up. "You say you hid when you heard the shots. Why?"

"Wait till I tell you," Mr Toman said. "When you hear shots around this country, you lie down. Many an innocent person was shot by the Army around here."

The Barrister was fuming. "Your Honour, you can't allow false allegations like this to be uttered in this court."

"Disregard that last statement," the judge told the Court Clerk.

Shane told Mr Toman he could stand down. "I'd like to call our last witness, Your Honour," Shane requested.

"Okay," the judge said, " but please make sure he makes no unqualified statements like your last witness."

"Okay, My Lord," Shane said. "I would like to call Mr John Wilson to the stand."

A tall, bald man got up and went to the stand. Kate didn't know him either. With the usual procedure carried out with the bible, Shane started questioning him. Most of this questioning was exactly the same as the last witness. When Shane asked him about his injury, he said he was still suffering slightly with it.

The Barrister stood up. "Have you ever had any compensation for the injury to your arm?" John Wilson said he hadn't. "I find it strange that if your arm was badly damaged, you wouldn't seek compensation."

"Because when I went to seek compensation, the police said there was no record of the incident." You knew the way John Wilson answered that he was raging about it.

The judge spoke up. "Seeing as there are no more witnesses on either side and the jury has heard the evidence of both sides, we will give them time to deliberate the whole case. There will be an adjournment of this court for two hours. Court will resume at two o'clock."

"All rise," the clerk said, and the judge left.

When they went outside, Tommy and Jenna were talking to some of the witnesses. Jenna told Kate they thought they had a great chance of winning. She said she knew one or two of the jurors from years ago at school and she knew they wouldn't side well with that Barrister.

Jenna suggested that they go for something to eat. They all went to Mellary's café, where they had tea and sandwiches. Tommy thought the evidence of Micky Toman and John Wilson was the winning of this case. They told the truth, and you can't beat the truth, and the fact that they corroborated each other's story would help a lot. They wandered back to the court, getting there at ten minutes to two. They went to their respective seats and waited for the second half.

Other people who left it late rushed in at the last minute so as not to offend the judge, as he seemed grumpy enough without being annoyed anymore.

On the dot of two o'clock, the clerk announced, "All rise." Sure enough, here he came. Sitting back up on his perch once again, he scanned around the court, looking over his glasses.

One would nearly think he was doing a recount to see if everyone was present. He started to talk. "In our two hours' recess, the jury has carefully considered all the evidence of this case. They have listened intently to all points made by both sides and I'm sure, as intelligent, fair and law-abiding people, they will give a fair and just verdict. I will call now on the Foreman of the Jury to deliver their verdict."

A small, well-dressed man in a navy suit and a dicky-bow tie stood up. You knew he was full of himself. "We, the members of the Jury, have studied all the evidence in this case. In the case of the evidence of the two unfortunate people who were injured, we must remember that they are seeking compensation, and this might taint their account of what happened."

Kate thought, *Is he saying we lied?*

The man went on, "The evidence of the two men who were working in the field was remarkable as they saw the incident as it happened and unfortunately suffered themselves because of it. Because of this and other important points we took into consideration, we find that John and Kate Grugan were unlawfully injured by British Forces and are entitled to full compensation. Especially in the case of Mr Grugan, who will carry this disability for the rest of his life." The man sat back down.

Kate smiled at John and caught his hand and squeezed it. She looked over at Jenna, who had a big grin on her face.

At that, the judge started to talk. "I would like to thank the jury for the way they conducted themselves today. A lot of points of law had to be carefully considered and I thought their contribution was tremendous. We now must respect their verdict. The court will adjourn for ten minutes until the amount of compensation is decided upon."

It seemed the longest ten minutes ever, with no one speaking. Everyone was either staring into space or looking at the floor. At last, he appeared.

"The compensation," he said. "In the case of Kate Grugan, there was a lot of time off work, plus the pain and the suffering a human being shouldn't have to suffer. We award you the sum of Thirty Thousand Pounds." Kate nearly fell off the seat.

He paused for a minute. "The case of John Grugan is an awful lot more serious, as he has a disability which he will carry for the rest of his life. This will leave him very limited in what he can do workwise. Therefore, in order to make sure he has enough financial backing to compensate for his lack of ability, we are awarding him the substantial sum of One Hundred and Fifty Thousand Pounds." The roar in the court was deafening. The judge banged his gavel on the bench. "Order in the court," he shouted twice. "Clear the court!" he then shouted. The court security men motioned everyone out of the building.

Kate threw her arms around John. They made their way out, where everybody was ecstatic. Tommy caught hold of Kate. "We matched the Brits on the battlefield and now we take their money. Jaysus, John, I'm absolutely delighted for you."

John was so excited. He turned to all the people who had come to support them and told them to be in Wheeler's tonight about eight o'clock. "Drinks are on me."

When they all went back to Mary's, she couldn't believe that they had won their case. "It's not often anyone comes out of court beating the Brits. Shane Gardner is responsible for that happening."

"He is some solicitor," Kate said.

That night, Jenna drove Tommy, Kate and John down to Wheeler's. The place was full. Everyone was in celebratory mood. John bought everyone a drink. They weren't home until the early hours.

The next couple of days they really enjoyed just hanging out with Mary, Jenna, Tommy and Baby Mary.

Some neighbours and friends called around to congratulate them on their success. Then Kate and John were due to go home tomorrow. Mary was usually in good form, but she was always feeling down when John and Kate were heading away. When they were saying their goodbyes, Mary just tapped both of them on the shoulder and went down to the room.

Chapter 41

Back in England, John and Kate worked away at their respective jobs. But things were changing slightly. In Kate's case, a lot of the barracks were closing due to the lack of people joining up, and a lot of the ones that remained, because of the lesser numbers, were using their own chefs to do the cooking. There was word of redundancies, but Kate, being one of the longest there, wasn't too worried as she thought she would be well down the list. But it wasn't to be.

When the first batch of redundancies was announced, she was on it. She was granted statutory redundancy. The money wasn't bothering her as she and John were financially sound from their compensation. What bothered her was that she had twenty years' service with the company and there were people kept who only had five- and six-years' service. She knew in her heart that she had been singled out because of her claim against the British Army.

John, on the other hand, loved his job from the moment he was appointed Office Manager.

But being Office Manager, one could see all the good points and bad points in the running of the company. All correspondence came through the office. Lately, he could see some of the contracts being cancelled. Letters demanding money were multiplying. And about twelve months after Kate was made redundant, John's company closed overnight. There weren't even redundancy payments.

As they were well enough off, John and Kate took a while to themselves and just relaxed. John would sometimes get a bit down, but Kate would cheer him up. But one morning Kate woke, and she felt desperately sick. She got sick a few times and John got annoyed. He told her he was taking her to the doctor.

When they reached the doctor's, there were three in front of her. They waited until it was Kate's turn, and she went on in and John remained in the waiting room. She seemed a long time in with the doctor and John wondered if there was really something seriously wrong, as she had been very sick that morning.

At last, he heard the surgery door opening and Kate came out. She had a grin on her face. John was puzzled. She came right up to him and looked him in the eye. "John, you are going to be a Daddy," she said, and she burst out crying. John was gobsmacked. He felt like crying, too.

For the next couple of weeks, they lived in a daze. They agreed they should tell no one for a month or so, just in case anything went wrong. The weeks went on and Kate's sickness got less and less. At the start of the second month, she was really flourishing and was awfully proud of her condition.

There were plenty of niggly wee rows as John was overprotective, not letting her even go walking on her own. He'd be trying to help her out of bed in the morning when she knew she was well able to get out herself. But, as time went on, John got less nervous about her and let her do her own thing.

She was about three months' pregnant when she let them know at home. Jenna would have got on the plane straight away, but she knew Tommy didn't want to go to England. Mary came on the phone. She was on it for nearly an hour, telling Kate what to do during pregnancy and what not to do. She told her in no uncertain terms not to do any hard work around the house and make sure John does it all. "And make him do it," she told her.

Her check-ups at the hospital were all fine and it was just a matter of waiting on the day.

John was looking forward to the Celtic game, and he had just settled down on the couch with a big mug of tea. The commentators were discussing the pros and cons of the game. John settled himself nicely into the couch as the referee blew the whistle for the kick-off. Just at that, Kate came into the room. She was slightly crouched over and awfully pale. "John, I have an awful pain," she said.

John leapt from the couch. "Here, Kate, sit down, sit down."

"No, John, I can't sit." She was sweating. The doctor had said the baby wasn't due for another week.

"Kate, we may go to the hospital. Wait till I find your bag." He threw the bag in the boot and came back and helped Kate slowly into the car. She looked wretched.

When they reached the hospital, Kate was just about able to walk into reception. When a nurse saw her, she brought a wheelchair and took Kate into the Maternity Ward.

John knew he had parked blocking an entry, and, seeing Kate in safe hands, he went to put the car in the car park. When he came back into the Maternity Ward, another nurse told him his wife had gone into labour. He walked up and down, and they didn't know how long he was doing this until the first nurse came out and took him into Kate. He thought she looked absolutely wrecked. She was holding the baby. It was wrapped in a blanket. He went over and hugged the two of them.

"It's a boy, John," she said. She handed him the child. He held on to him so tight. He stared at his little face. *What a brilliant day*, he thought.

Kate was dozing off, and when the nurse came in to check on her, she said to John it might be better if he left and let Kate get some sleep. He agreed. "We'll look after the baby until she's able to," the nurse said. "Unless you want to take it with you," she joked.

"No, no!" John said. "I think he'd be better here."

"Come as early as you like in the morning," she said.

John was home before he knew it. His head was all over the place. He made himself a cup of tea, but threw half of it out. He'd better ring home. It was Jenna who answered the call. John told her the good news and he could hear her shouting to Tommy, telling him it was a boy. She told him to tell Kate they were delighted. She said Mary had gone down to one of the neighbours and she would be delighted when she heard the news.

The phone rang the next morning. John looked at the clock. Six thirty. *Jesus*, he thought, *there's something wrong at the hospital.* Nervously, he answered the phone.

"John," he heard, "it's your mother. I couldn't wait any longer." She was crying. "John, I am absolutely delighted for you and Kate. How are her and the baby doing?"

He told her how he had only seen them for a short while last night, but the nurse said they were both okay. They talked on for a while, and she seemed more settled when she went off the phone.

John lay in for a while, and when he got up he tidied up a bit as there was stuff all over the place as they had left in such a hurry yesterday to get to the hospital. He was just about to go to the hospital when the phone rang. It was Meabh. She wanted to know how Kate was and the weight of the baby.

Again, John explained that he only had a short time with Kate last night, but he was going in there now and he would find all that out and he would let them all know. They said their goodbyes and John headed for the hospital. On his way, he called into the flower shop across from the supermarket and he bought the biggest bunch of roses he could find. He asked the lady for a nice card for his wife on the birth of their new baby.

She showed him a few different ones and he picked the one he thought she would like best.

When he got to the hospital, Kate had the baby lying on the bed, trying to figure out which Babygro to put on him. When John came in and gave Kate the flowers and the card, she threw her arms around him and gave him a big kiss. She picked the baby up and told John to sit on the armchair, and then placed the baby in his arms. He felt so proud. They both just sat there looking at the baby.

"Did you think of any names, John?" Kate asked him.

He felt a bit stupid as with all the commotion he hadn't even thought about names. "God, no; sorry, Kate, I never thought about names."

She said, "Well, I would like to call him after you, John; and another reason I want to call him John is that John Carter possibly saved your life when he drove you to the hospital."

John looked down at the baby. "My man, you have just been christened John," he said.

Kate and John sat talking and she dressed the baby. He asked how she was, and she told him she felt a bit weak, but that would pass, and she didn't mind as long as the baby was okay. A nurse came in with tea, and when she saw the flowers, she thought they were lovely. She left and came back almost immediately with a vase of water which she put the flowers in and placed them on the bedside locker.

Kate was glad to get home as, apart from John and her parents and a couple of neighbours, she hadn't had too many visitors.

Chapter 42

Kate and the baby had been home now for a couple of weeks. She and John had just got used to the middle-of-the-night feeds. It was all new to them. After a while, things got a lot easier. They were sitting talking one night when John said that he'd love to take the baby home to show him to his mother. Kate thought it a great idea and said to John, "Why don't we get him christened in Ireland?"

John thought she was joking. "No," she said, "I love Ireland. They would have all his family there and she thought she could persuade her Mum and Dad to come, too.

She rang her mother that evening and asked them to come over for tea. They were delighted. After tea, her Mum and Dad were nursing the child between them. Kate thought the time was right. "Mum and Dad," she said, "we have something to ask you both." John stayed quiet. "We are thinking of having the baby christened in John's parish church in Ireland, but we would want the two of you to be there. Would you come?"

One looked at the other. Kate wondered if she had done the right thing. At that, her father spoke. "What a great idea! The last time we were in Ireland, we both loved the Guinness. But you will have to help us book accommodation."

"Don't worry about that," Kate said. "We'll get you sorted." They were delighted.

The next evening, Kate rang to tell Jenna her plan. Jenna thought it was a brilliant idea and she said she would go over to see Fr Seamus when she was off the phone. She asked Kate if she had any preferable dates. Kate said she hadn't and would take whatever date was available.

Jenna rang back the next evening to tell Kate that she had provisionally booked this Sunday three weeks with Fr Seamus and wondered if that would suit her. Kate said yes, she would take it. She asked her if she could help book somewhere for her Mum and Dad to stay for a few days, as they were coming over for the christening. Jenna laughed. "That will be easily sorted," she told Kate. "Myself and Tommy have just moved in to our new house and there is ample room there for your mother and father."

Kate couldn't get over this offer. She thanked Jenna for all her help, telling her she'd keep in touch.

John and Kate and her mother and father travelled over to Ireland the Thursday before the christening. This gave them plenty of time to fulfil any arrangements that had to be taken care of with Fr Seamus. He was a young priest, and since taking over as Parish Priest, he seemed to be getting on better than his predecessor. John and Kate had a meeting with him in the parochial house on the Friday evening. It was very formal and the whole arrangement was professionally carried out in a very short time.

Meabh and Paul travelled up on the Saturday. The one thing that Kate thought great was the way John's family welcomed her Mum and Dad. Mary even insisted that they come to bingo with her on the Friday. Kate thought her mother was reluctant enough, but was very happy when she came home having won Forty Pounds.

Tommy and Jenna were over the moon on the day as they were standing for the baby. Jenna was in her glory, carrying the baby into the chapel with Tommy by her side.

The ceremony took less than half an hour and they headed over to Creedon's Hotel for a meal. They invited Fr Seamus and he said he would follow on after he had finished in the church.

The meal was first class, and after a while Mary and Kate's mother and father decided they'd go home. Mary told Kate she would take little John home and look after him if Kate wanted to stay on for a few drinks. Kate said maybe she could go home. But Mary insisted. "I am sure myself and your mother and father will be well able to mind a small baby. Now away on and enjoy yourself." Mary took the baby and Jenna drove them all home. She got a taxi back and told Kate how her sister was minding Baby Mary overnight and she was taking the opportunity to let her hair down. It was late when they called the taxi, and everyone was glad to get home.

Little John let out a cry at seven the next morning. Kate woke in a daze. Realising where she was, she rolled out of bed.

"Do you want me to get the bottle?" John asked. She didn't know why he asked, as he was well wrapped up in the blankets and showed no sign of moving.

You would think little John was jealous that she was out last night, as he kept spitting out the bottle. She eventually got him fed and changed and she put him back in the cot. She decided to get up. Mary was already in the kitchen, making tea and toast for Kate's mother and father. Jenna was feeding little Mary over on the couch.

It then dawned on Kate that her parents had to be driven to the airport as they were returning home today. They told Kate that they had really enjoyed their day yesterday and were really glad they had come. When Kate went back down to the room to check on the baby, John was in the shower. The baby was sound asleep, so she went back to the kitchen and had her breakfast.

It was one o'clock and it was time for Kate and John to drive her parents back to the airport. They all said their goodbyes and Kate set off driving. When they got to the airport, Kate and John accompanied her parents to the check-in. As they were saying their goodbyes, Kate's mother took an envelope from her handbag and handed it to Kate. "Sorry, Kate, we never got a chance to give that to little John. You will be able to get him something nice." Kate and John thanked them, and they were off.

On the way back home, curiosity got the better of Kate. She opened the envelope that her parents had given her. It contained a beautiful card with two angel figures dressed in blue on the front. She opened the card and the notes fell on to her lap. "My God!" she said. She picked up the notes and counted them. "Five Hundred Pounds," she said. "My God, that is too much."

"They obviously think he is worth it," John said.

When they got back to Mary's, Paul and Meabh were there and they were ready to head back. Meabh said she wanted to get back home as she was missing wee Seamus. They said they had really enjoyed the christening and they should get together more often.

They said their goodbyes and they were on their way.

John and Kate said they'd hang around for another few days and Mary was delighted, as she loved looking after little John. Kate couldn't believe how much she herself loved it around here and how she hated it when she had first come.

Chapter 43

It was the following Thursday morning when Kate took the child into the kitchen to prepare his bottle. Mary was sitting by the stove. Kate said good morning to her, but there was no answer. Kate thought she hadn't heard her. She asked her if she wanted to hold the child, but she said she was finishing her tea. Kate thought this very strange, as she would usually take the child off Kate when she came into the kitchen.

John had wanted to visit an old school friend and to show him the new baby. On the way, Kate asked John if he had noticed anything strange about his mother that morning. He said he hadn't really been talking to her as she was down in the room when he got up.

It was a good drive, and by the time they got there and back they were away almost the whole day. When they got back that evening, Mary wasn't in the kitchen or sitting room. They thought this strange because no one got through Mary's door without her greeting them.

John was worried and he said he'd check the bedroom. He rapped the door and went in. To his surprise, Mary was in bed. "Ma, you're in bed early. What's wrong?" he asked.

She didn't turn around. "Just a bit tired," was all she said. He went back up to tell Kate.

"I'll make her a cup of tea," Kate said.

Kate went down with the tea and was leaving it on the locker when she saw Mary's face. She shouted up to John. "John, ring an ambulance at once."

John headed to the room to see what was wrong. Kate nearly knocked him down as she raced into the kitchen. "We need a fucking ambulance – your mother's taking a stroke."

John ran to the room. His mother was a terrible colour. Her jaw seemed to have dropped to one side. John didn't know what to do. He went back up to the kitchen. "Kate, Kate, what will we do, what will we do?"

"Settle, John; help is on its way," Kate told him. "All we can do is keep her comfortable."

In a short time, they heard a vehicle driving fast into the yard. It was a paramedic in a Jeep. He jumped out with his medical bag. "Where is the patient?" he asked Kate, running to the house. "Time is vital in this case," he said.

Kate took him straight to Mary's room. He started working on her straight away. It wasn't long after when the ambulance arrived with its sirens blazing. Baby John woke with the noise. John lifted him in his arms to console him. Kate showed the ambulance men to the bedroom. After working on Mary for about twenty minutes, one of the ambulance men went out and came back in with a trolley bed. They whisked her to the hospital in record time.

Kate went down to the room and the paramedic was clearing up all the medical paraphernalia that had been used. John came into the room still holding the child. "What's the situation?" he asked. "How bad is she?"

"With a stroke," the paramedic said, "it's all about time, and you were lucky I was at another call-out just about a mile away. I got here in good time and that might stand to her."

"Is there any point in going to see her tonight?" Kate asked.

"I would advise against it as she will be in Intensive Care, and you mightn't be able to see her. But there should be no bother tomorrow getting in to see her."

Kate and John thanked the paramedic and he said he hoped she was going to be all right.

Jenna and Tommy burst through the door just after the paramedic had left. John told them that their mother had taken a stroke. Tommy said that John Dinsmore had passed by here a while ago and had seen the ambulance and paramedic's Jeep and rang him to see what was wrong. "Jesus Christ," Tommy said. "And she looked so well at the christening."

Kate told them she never answered her this morning when she asked her if she wanted to feed the child. "That's not like her," she said. "And then when she was in bed when we came home, it set off the alarm bells. But at least help got here very quickly."

Jenna said wee Mary was asleep in the car and she'd better go out and take her in, and Kate said she'd make Baby John a bottle as he was overdue one with all the commotion. John knew Tommy was very annoyed and assured him that the paramedic had told him that she had a good chance of a recovery because they got there so quickly to attend to her.

Jenna said they should hold off ringing Meabh until morning as there was no point in annoying her tonight. She said she'd ring her first thing in the morning.

John said he would go to the hospital in the morning to see what the position was, and he would let them know straight away. Tommy and Jenna went off home.

The next morning, about eleven o'clock, John arrived at the hospital. He was directed to the Stroke Ward. He asked the nurse at the desk where he could find Mary Grugan. She went through the file and said she was in Ward Eight. She got up and said she would take him there. On the way, she told him that Mary would have trouble talking to him. When he went in, he saw Mary propped up with two pillows behind her. She looked very pale, and he gave her a big hug. She tried to talk, but her speech was very slurred, and he could barely make out what she was saying. She pulled at the dressing gown the hospital had put her in and pointed to it with her other hand, and he figured that she wanted her own dressing gown and pyjamas. She was then pulling at her hair and pointing, and this told him she wanted her own hairbrush. At least she was alert enough to be able to tell him this in her own way. He told her he would go home and get Kate to gather up her essentials and she would probably be in with them herself this evening. Mary just put her thumb up. After a while, she dozed off to sleep and John decided that was the time to go.

On the way, he went back to reception and asked to see someone who was dealing with his mother. The nurse went off and after a while came back with a man dressed in a suit. He told John he was the person dealing with his mother. He said she had suffered a mild stroke. "As you can see," he said, "her speech is affected and could be for some time. But the fact that she got medical help so quickly will definitely stand to her." He also added it could be a couple of weeks before they would see any great change in her. John thanked the doctor for his explanation and headed for home.

When Kate heard the car pulling into the yard, she went to the door to hear John's news. He told her everything the doctor told him, and he said he was happy himself with what he had heard. He also told her that his mother wanted night clothes and a hairbrush and showed Kate how she told him she wanted them. John said maybe she'd organise them and take them in to her this evening. Kate said she'd ring Jenna to come over and they would gather up all she wanted.

Jenna came over and they went to Mary's room and gathered up all they thought she would need. They actually decided to take a complete change of clothes for her. Jenna said Kathleen Tate's daughter was coming over at seven o'clock to mind the baby and she and Tommy were going to the hospital at that time, and if Kate was ready, they would call for her and they could all go together.

When they reached the hospital and went to Mary's ward, Jenna thought Tommy was going to break down crying. He threw his arms around her and held on for a long time. When he came away from her, Jenna could see the tears in his eyes. Jenna and Kate both hugged her, and just at that, she started pulling at the dressing gown and pointing to her hair. Jenna thought this was so funny. Kate then opened the bag and showed her the clothes inside. Mary tried to smile, but her jaw dropped to one side.

Kate suggested to Tommy that if he stood back she and Jenna could pull the curtains around the bed and give Mary a complete change of clothes and brush her hair. He did, and they did just that. It brought Kate back to the time she was doing it for John when he was in hospital.

When they opened the curtains again, Mary gestured for Tommy to come and sit beside her. He gave her a big hug. They could see she was a lot happier in her own clothes.

After a while, they left. Tommy and Jenna dropped Kate home and she was mad to see John and to see how he had gotten on with the baby, as it was his first time being on his own with him.

When she got into the house, John was sitting nursing the baby when he should long have been asleep. She smiled and took the baby off John to put him in his cot. John got up and made two cups of coffee and they sat down. John wanted to know how his mother was.

As they were talking, they heard a car coming very fast into the yard. At that, the door opened. In came Meabh. When she saw them, she burst into tears. Kate sat her in the armchair. "How is Mam?" she asked. "Is she going to die?"

John said he didn't think she would. He explained how they found her and lucky enough there was a paramedic close by, and how they got her into hospital quickly, and that was in her favour.

Meabh told them that she had been on her own when she got the word as Paul was away at an Agricultural Show in Germany for a few days. She was that eager to come up to see her mother, Paul's sister said she'd look after the baby. Kate gave her a cup of coffee and tried to get her to calm down. They talked for a while, but the long journey had taken its toll on Meabh and she said she was going to bed.

Kate and John sat talking and they agreed that they would have to stay around here another while as it wouldn't be right to go back to England with his mother in hospital in case anything went wrong.

The next day, Meabh was mad to get to see her Mam. She could hardly wait until visiting time. She asked Kate what Mary needed most. Kate told Meabh that she and Jenna had taken in most of what she needed the night before. Meabh said she would go to the shop and get her some reading material. Kate knew Mary wouldn't be able to read, but she didn't want to put Meabh in any worse form than she was, so she let her go ahead.

Kate told John that maybe he should go with Meabh to see his mother, and John joked that she didn't trust him with the child. John and Meabh headed off and arrived at the hospital just at visiting time. Meabh had the magazines in a bag for her mother. When they entered the ward, Mary was staring in their direction but didn't seem to recognise them. When they got up beside her, she kind of smiled at them. Meabh burst out crying and went to her mother and squeezed her tight. She couldn't contain herself from crying. John put his arm around her.

"Oh, Jesus, she's desperate-looking," Meabh whispered to John. John assured her that she looked a bit better than she did the night before.

They stayed until the end of visiting time and they both gave her a hug and left, letting her know there would be someone to see her that night.

Chapter 44

Kate had rung her parents to tell them about Mary
having the stroke and that they would be staying
in Ireland for some while. She asked them if they
would keep a check on the house, and they said
they'd be delighted to. She asked them to check
the postbox.

The next day, her father rang back and told
her that everything was all right at the house. He
said there was a letter in the postbox addressed to
John. He told her it had Coldsworth Prosthetic
Clinic typed on the top of the envelope. Kate was
puzzled and she told him to open it. He read it
out to her:

"An appointment has been arranged for
John Grugan to have his permanent prosthetic
limb tested and fitted on Tuesday 27th May.
Would you please let us know if this day suits
you?"

Kate asked her dad for the phone number of the clinic. He read it out and she took note of it. She thanked him and told him she'd be in touch.

John was a bit sceptical about going to get a new limb as he said the one he had was working well enough, although he thought this is the end of the whole procedure and he'd better go along with it. Kate rang straight away and booked the appointment.

Meabh had rung Paul's sister to see if it would be okay to leave the baby with her another night as she would like to visit her mother again tomorrow. Paul's sister said there was no bother as her own bigger two were taking turns walking the baby in the pram and fighting over who would feed him next. She said there wasn't a bother on wee Seamus, and she told her to stay another night surely.

She asked her how her mother was, and when Meabh told her how she was, she told her to be in no rush home.

Meabh was just off the phone when it rang again. John answered it and handed it to Meabh. "It's Paul for you, Meabh."

Paul had wondered why she wasn't at home when he rang the house. When he rang his mother's, thinking Meabh might be there, his mother related the whole story about Mary taking the stroke and Meabh heading up to see her. Paul said, "I am so sorry about your mother, Meabh. Jesus, this is desperate, and I can't get home until the end of the week. How is she and how are you coping?"

She told him about his sister Bridget keeping the child and her driving up to see her mother. She told him she saw Mary last night and she didn't look good. She also told him she had asked Bridget if she would keep the child another night and she said she was only too delighted to. Paul said he felt terrible being that far away and not being able to help. He told her to keep her head up and her mother would be alright. Then he told her he loved her and the phone went dead.

John asked Meabh and Kate if they would like a takeaway for tea as he was buying. They both said they'd love a takeaway. Kate said she would love a Cod and Chips and Meabh said she'd have the same. He was just about to leave when Meabh said, "Sure, I'll go with you for the spin."

On the way, she told John how she was missing Paul for a bit of support right now. But she was also glad that he hadn't missed the show in Germany as it had been booked for over twelve months and he had been really looking forward to it. "Who's going in to see Mam tonight?" she asked, as she said she would like to go.

John said Tommy and Jenna were going in and he said he'd ring them when he got back and tell them to pick her up.

When they got back home, John rang Jenna and told them to pick Meabh up on their way to the hospital. They all enjoyed the takeaway, and it wasn't long after that Tommy and Jenna arrived, and they were on their way to see Mary.

Tommy, Jenna and Meabh arrived back after an hour or so. Meabh had some of Mary's used clothes home with her. "I'll put them in the washing if you don't mind, Kate, and the nurse said because I'm travelling such a long journey tomorrow, I can have an early visit in the morning."

"You might have an early visit okay, but you're not starting to wash clothes tonight. I'll wash those clothes in the morning and have them ready for tomorrow evening. You have enough on your plate."

Tommy and Jenna headed for home. Kate felt a wee nightcap might help them all to sleep. They talked for a while, and they all went to bed.

The next day, Kate cooked them all a good breakfast. After breakfast, Meabh told them that after she went in to visit her mother in the hospital she wouldn't be coming back to the house as it was a long journey and she wanted to get on the road early. She asked them to keep her well informed about her mother's condition and they promised they would. They waved her off.

Chapter 45

This was the week that John had to go over to England, and it had been arranged that if he had to stay overnight, he would stay with Kate's mother and father. Kate would have loved to have brought the child over, but he was too young, and it was uncertain how long John would have to remain there. John was happy enough to go on his own, and thankfully in the end he was only the one day in the clinic, but he decided to stay overnight in Kate's mother and father's house so he could go over and check their own house and get a flight home the next day.

As the weeks went by, Mary started to improve. She even started walking with the aid of two walking sticks. When John visited, he used to teach her wee tricks that he learned when he was going through his own rehabilitation. Sometimes, Kate thought John was pushing her too hard, but he made the point that if he hadn't been pushed he never would have got to where he was today. Mary was eventually walking with the aid of one stick; slowly, but she was getting there. One of her legs wasn't great, and John used to kid her to get it cut off and get a prosthetic one like his. She used to threaten him with the walking stick when he said this to her. But Kate could see this sort of crack was keeping her spirits up.

Meabh and Paul had been up to see Mary a good few times since Paul came back from Germany. When Paul saw her for the first time, he couldn't get over how frail she was. But lately, himself and Meabh thought she had improved immensely.

It was one Monday evening when John and Kate had just arrived in the ward for the visit. Mary's speech had well improved, and she couldn't wait to tell them her good news. "I'm getting home tomorrow. What do you think of that?" she said. Kate and John were taken by surprise. They didn't know what to say. "Are you not happy for me?" she said.

"Of course we are happy for you," Kate said. "We just didn't think you would be out for a while yet."

"You don't know how happy we are that you're coming home," John said.

Kate said she'd go and talk to someone about Mary coming home. John stayed with his mother.

When Kate got to the reception, she asked the nurse if there was any word of Mary Grugan being let out. The nurse looked at her file. "Yes," she said. "The stroke specialist is visiting Mary tomorrow and if she has had no setback, he is definitely letting her go home. Now," she added, "there will be a special programme to be undertaken and she will have a package home with her that will explain everything." She went on to tell Kate that Mary will have to attend a mobility clinic to try and improve her walking.

Kate told her she understood, as her husband had lost part of his leg and she understood exactly what has to happen. Kate then gave the nurse her phone number and asked her if she would give her a ring when Mary was getting out and they could come and collect her. The nurse said as soon as she got the word, she'd ring her.

Kate went back to the ward. "Ah, it seems you're coming home to us tomorrow, Mary. We'll have to get the flags out, my girl," she said.

"Jesus, I'll be glad to get home," Mary said. "They are very nice people here, but I would rather be at home."

Kate told Mary how the nurse would ring them and let them know when she was ready for home. They left relieved, knowing they wouldn't have to visit Mary here anymore.

You think the weatherman knew Mary was getting home. It was a beautiful day. Kate had picked out clothes for Mary that she thought she would like and put them in a small case in the boot of the car and waited for the phone call. It was now one o'clock and Kate thought it wouldn't be long now. But two, three and four o'clock went by and no phone call. Kate thought that perhaps she wasn't getting out after all. She would be very disappointed. *Why did they build up her hopes?* It had now just gone past five o'clock. *No chance now*, Kate thought to herself. *Mary's going to be in some form tonight when we go to see her.*

Just at that, the phone rang. "Hello," Kate said.

"Kate Grugan?" the woman said.

"Yes," Kate answered.

"Mrs Grugan, this is the nurse from the hospital. I want to apologise; we've had a terrible delay at the hospital today and we fell way behind. Mary was the last patient to be seen in the Stroke Ward. But the good news is she is going home."

"Oh, that's great news," Kate said. "We will be in straight away. Thanks for ringing." She shouted to John that his mother was coming home. She told him to ring Tommy and Jenna, as they wanted to be there when she came home, and they could keep an eye on the baby. Kate had her coat on and was ready to go when Jenna and Tommy arrived shortly after John came off the phone. They headed to the car, and they were off.

When they got to the ward, Mary was standing at the door in her dressing gown. "I thought I wasn't getting out today," she said. "Come on!" and she was heading for the car.

"Hold on, Mary," Kate said. "I have clothes here for you to change into and I'll go to the bathroom with you and help you."

"That's a good idea," John said, hoping she'd agree.

She turned and headed in the direction of the bathroom and Kate held on to her arm to steady her. John found a bag and collected the contents of her locker into it. They would be ready to go when his Ma was dressed.

When Kate and Mary returned, the three of them headed for the car. It took Mary a long time to reach the car. Kate didn't mind, as John used to be the same when he first came out of hospital. John helped his mother into the back seat, and when they got home Tommy came out. He and John almost carried her into the house.

Jenna had tea and sandwiches for everyone. She had young Mary and John asleep in their prams. Mary hobbled over to the prams and kissed both kids. She stumbled. Tommy went to her aid and sat her in the armchair beside the fire. John rang Meabh to tell her that Mary had got out of hospital and was doing fine. Word had got out that Mary was back home, and many of her neighbours called to see her. A very busy night.

Chapter 46

Over the next few weeks, Mary made great strides. She and John went walking every day. John used to tease her that if she went much faster, she'd be passing him out, and she found the special classes great help, and her general health was improving. Mary hadn't taken a drink since she came home. She was partial to a small drink from time to time. She had recently started to go back to bingo. Mary Gray and her husband Jim called every week and helped her to get there.

It was one night when Kate and John had just finished watching a film. Mary had just come in the door from bingo. She said she had no luck, but enjoyed the night. Mary had taken her coat and scarf off and hung them in the hall. When she came back into the kitchen, Kate thought she looked puzzled, and she asked her if she wanted a cup of tea. Mary sort of smiled at them. She went over to the cupboard and produced the bottle. "Long time since I had one of these. Will you join me?"

John got up, helped her sit down in the armchair and took the bottle from her. He went and got the glasses and a mixer and poured three drinks. He gave his Mam and Kate their drinks and sat down with his own.

"Plenty of reason to celebrate tonight, Ma, with you back home."

"Yes, indeed," Kate said.

"There's no better reason for celebrating than that," Mary said.

John and Kate wondered what she meant. She said nothing for what seemed a lifetime. Kate and John were waiting. She turned to face them. "I have spoken to Tommy and Meabh and they agree with me. I am going to need help from now on to live my life to the full. I need someone full-time to assist me. Kate, I know you hated this place when you came to it, but I know now you are a brilliant person. I look at the way you cared for John. He would never have recovered as well only for you. John, I look at you and I see how strong you were to recover so well, and then the way you pushed me to get as good as I am. Well, I want to ask you both. Pour the three of us another drink, John."

She stopped talking then. Kate was wondering what was coming next. John rushed to get the drinks poured to hear what she was going to say. They waited. She took a large drink

317

from her glass. "I want you two to come and live with me here and you will have this house when I pass on."

Kate and John looked at each other. They didn't know what to say. The room went silent.

"Now," Mary said, "I know I'm after giving you both a shock and it would be a pretty big decision on your behalf, and you must make up your own mind; but I have just told you what I would like to happen.

"Obviously you're not going to discuss it while I'm present," Mary said. "But take your time to think about it and make your own decision. Good night. I'm off to bed."

Kate went down to the room with her and returned to the kitchen when she was safely tucked in.

John just looked at Kate and asked her what she thought. "I don't know what to think," Kate said.

"I don't think you would want to leave England for good, would you, Kate?"

"John, I have got to love it over here and I think your mother is a brilliant person, but there's other things to think of. We would have to sell the house in England and get all our bits and pieces sorted out. The only real problem is my Mum and Dad, as they would be left on their own; but their plan is to retire into a Retirement

Village anyway. They have all the arrangements put in place for that already; and anyway, it's not too far away to visit them regularly. But, anyway, John, we'll talk about it no more tonight. Let's wake up with fresh heads in the morning and see how we feel then."

Kate and John discussed it over and over. They discussed it with Tommy and Meabh, and they both assured them they were behind the idea. Then one morning as they were driving into town to get a few groceries, John said he enjoyed the easy-going life in Ireland compared to the traffic congestion in England.

"That's it," Kate said. "We are coming here to live with your mother."

"Are you sure, Kate?" John said.

"Stop, stop!" Kate said. "That's the decision made. We'll talk no more about it."

The crunch came when they had to inform Kate's parents of their plan. They decided that the best way to do it was to go over and visit them for a weekend. About two weeks later, Kate, John and the baby headed for England. Kate's parents were all over the baby. They even suggested on the Saturday evening that Kate and John visit the Seamen's Lodge for a few beers, and they would mind the child until they came back. They went down to the Seamen's Lodge, but didn't stay too long as they were worried how Kate's Mum and Dad would handle the child at their ages. What didn't help was a crowd of drunken British soldiers who had just returned from a foreign tour of duty, who were very drunk and kicking up a racket in the pub. Kate looked at John, nodding at the soldiers. "We'll be a lot happier in Ireland." John smiled.

When they got back to Kate's mother and father's, they were both trying to settle little John. "We tried everything," Kate's Mum said. "He won't stop crying."

Kate took him in her arms and cuddled him, and you would think he knew it was his mother. After a while, Kate made him a bottle and gave him to her mother to feed. She was in her glory. Kate then put him down for the night. Kate's father remarked that they hadn't stayed too long in the pub. Kate explained to him about the soldiers being there and how they were getting rowdy, and they thought it better to leave.

"In other words, you had your drink spoiled," Kate's Dad said. "Well, we can't have that," he said. He went over to the cabinet in the sitting room and produced a bottle. "I got this the last time I was in Gran Canaria. We always like company when we are drinking," he said.

He poured four drinks, and they started talking. "You know, Kate," he said. "It's a long time since we had a drink together. With you being in Ireland so much over this last while, myself and your mum were thinking you were going to move over there. I was cutting your grass the other day and it came into my head that soon I'll not be able to do this, and we might have to hire someone to do that job. Anyway, when we move into the Retirement Village, we will be too far away to travel that far."

Kate looked at John. *Now is the time to tell them*, she thought. At that, her father got up and got them another drink. When he settled back down, Kate started. "Mum and Dad, when me and John came over this weekend, we had something we wanted to discuss with you both." They gave her a puzzled look. "Since John's mother came out of hospital, she has needed a lot of help. The other night when we were sitting having a chat, she started telling us how vulnerable she felt and how much she depended on us – and out of the blue she asked us to move in with her.

"She told us that when she passes on, she was leaving her house to us." Her mother and father looked at her, but said nothing.

John started, "Look, folks, Kate is worried that if this situation happens, you will think she is abandoning you two. But we wouldn't do that, as it takes very little effort to get over here, and we would come over regularly. We would like to hear what you both think."

Kate's Mum and Dad looked at each other but said nothing for a few minutes. It was Kate's mother who spoke up. "Kate, we were also going to have a heart-to-heart with you two as things are going to drastically change for us, as we are planning to sell up here and go to live at the Retirement Village as soon as possible, as we are finding it hard to keep the gardens here the way we want them. We reckon we would be better going there while we are still able to enjoy ourselves. The money we get from the sale of the house will easily keep us for the rest of our lives, and you two will get whatever is left," she said, smiling.

"I am looking forward to using the Mini Golf Course they have there," Kate's father said, laughing. "But you bring young John to see us regularly."

"And you will be able to come and stay with us on holidays," Kate said. "Baby John would love to see you any time."

Kate's dad got them another drink. "We always knew you would end up in Ireland, Kate," her mother said.

They sat for a while talking until they all decided it was time to go to bed. Kate knew she would sleep soundly as things had worked out so well with her Mum and Dad.

Chapter 47

When they got back to Ireland, Mary said how much she had missed not having them about, and she said that if it wasn't for the fact that Jenna had come over every day to help her she mightn't have been able to stay on her own.

"Look, Mary," Kate said, "I have good news for you; myself and John are going to come and live here and there won't be a bother on you."

Mary was overcome with emotion and Kate told her to sit down in the chair and gave her wee John to divert her attention from starting to cry. "God, he's getting so big," Mary said. "You know, Kate, we are going to have such a great time when we are all together. I hope I live long enough to see this fellow starting school."

"Don't be silly, Mary," Kate said. "You could live to see him getting married."

Mary burst out laughing. "You must think I'm going to live forever, Kate."

"Ma," John said, "we intend to sell our house in England and myself and Kate were wondering if you would mind if we did a bit of improvement to this house."

Kate butted in. "Mary, we don't mean that there's much wrong with your house. We thought that we might do up our bedroom and the room for the child and maybe modernise the bathroom."

Mary told them, "Do whatever you want. I have the money to do these things. But I don't want you to touch my bedroom, as Seamus papered that room before he passed away and it will stay that way until I pass on."

Kate and John were very busy, what with them trying to sell their own house and helping Kate's mother and father to sell theirs. With their compensation money they were able to start the improvements to Mary's house almost straight away.

Eventually, their house sold, as did Kate's parents' house. Kate and John spent a couple of weeks in England, helping them to move into the Retirement Village. They took whatever stuff they wanted to keep, and Kate took anything she wanted, and they auctioned off the rest. Kate was happy herself as her parents seemed to be set on living out the rest of their lives in this Retirement Village.

As usual when they got back to Mary's, she was delighted to see them. She told them she h a d won the jackpot of £100 last Friday night. "Go down to my room and bring me up the parcel on the bed, please," she asked Kate. She opened the parcel when Kate brought it to her. "I hope these fit the wee man," she said. "Jenna took me shopping the other day and I decided to spend my winnings on him."

"Mary, we'll find out now when I feed and change him and we'll put one of these new outfits on him," Kate said. "They are all lovely."

All the work was done to the house and Kate and John were well settled and young John was getting bigger. Meabh, Paul and young Seamus would come up and stay fairly regularly. Tommy was immersed in the political drive to get candidates selected for the local elections, with Jenna by his side as usual. John had taken a good interest in the political situation. He thought the way things were going with the Peace Process was far better than the old days with all the troubles. He was even persuaded to deliver leaflets around the doors when Tommy put the pressure on him. Kate would help out with whatever Tommy asked her to do.

Young John and Mary were at school now. Their Granny had got to see her wish come true, and while she lived another couple of years, Mary succumbed to old age and passed away in her sleep one night. How history was to repeat itself. The next morning after Mary had passed away, Pat Dunne came with a tricolour and placed it on the lid of the coffin in Mary's room where she was waked. He told Tommy and John to let him know the arrangements for the funeral, as their mother would be getting a Guard of Honour from the house to the grave, just like her husband Seamus did. The boys thanked him. Pat turned to Tommy and joked, "The only thing that will be missing will be the firing of the shots." They all laughed.

The next few weeks, Kate and John felt the house was very quiet. Even young John mentioned how he missed his Granny. Kate had more time to herself now and she said to John she might go over to see her mother and father for a few days. She decided to go on her own, and that way John could get young John out to school every day. She booked into digs beside the Retirement Village and spent most of the day with them. They had settled in very well with their own little apartment. They seemed very happy, but she thought her mother was a very bad colour. She didn't say anything. She returned home and told John what she thought. He was quick to dismiss it, saying maybe she had a bug of some kind. But she knew he was only saying that to stop her from worrying.

Six months later, her mother passed away from some virus which they couldn't find a cure for. Kate and John had sat with her the whole week before she passed away. Jenna took young John and went over for the funeral, as Tommy was still anxious about travelling to England.

When the funeral was over, Kate's dad was very down in himself. John suggested that Kate should stay on for a while and he would go home with young John and Jenna, as young John had exams the following week.

She remained in England for a couple of weeks, spending every day with her father. That year she visited him a lot, but just after Christmas he passed away. Kate knew he never got over her mother's death and he probably died of a broken heart in the end. Kate realised her ties with England were at last gone.

Young John was doing well at college now. He was studying politics and history. So was his cousin Mary. His Uncle Tommy was loving this as he kept telling the two of them that while years ago they had taken on the Brits militarily, the young people would now be able to take them on politically.

It was many years later, on a lovely sunny day, when Kate and John were having their lunch at the patio table in the yard. Kate was sitting back, sipping a cup of coffee and scanning the beautiful countryside in front of her and thinking how she hated this place when she first came here all those years ago. The telegraph pole outside the gate came into her view and the photo of her own son with the caption: 'Vote Sinn Féin, Vote John Grugan No 1.' John had won a seat in the assembly, and to cap it all, his cousin Mary had won a seat in the next constituency. Kate and John were absolutely delighted. But not as delighted as Tommy Grugan.